E.O.L

(End of Life)

The Clear Conspiracy

Revised Edition

Art Jetthree

To the memory of my sister, Jeanine, and

my first true love, Deborah Ann Brodie.

Last but not least,

my beloved Grandmother,

Gladys Woodson.

You have all given me the courage to be a wonderfully imperfect man empowered with integrity to live a life committed to helping others.

Thank you to my mother, Harriet Woodson, for bringing me into this world and teaching me that perfection is a nebulous non-entity and frivolous state of being. A special appreciation to my friend, Andy Luria, for being a wise spirit and empowering my writing journey. Finally, thank you, Jean Maldonado, for believing, sharing in my dreams, and helping to pave the way.

Table of Contents

Preface

The Clear Conspiracy is the first book of the E.O.L. (End of Life) trilogy. It introduces the story of Jay Preston, a talented and uniquely gifted hospice social worker, who becomes an unwitting player and victim in a deadly conspiracy of epidemic proportions. A decaying war-ravaged planet Earth is the backdrop of a divided world engulfed in classism, racism, and greed. A battlefield centered in New York City pits a determined few against organized, ruthless, powerful individuals, and public institutions willing to slaughter millions of innocent people in an all-out murder spree to gain money and power. Jay uncovers an unearthly source of the conspiracy and suffers great losses in his struggle to survive. The victor will create a pattern of new beginnings for American and global society.

Chapter I: One Day at a Time

New York City - January

"No…no, I'm not all right, okay? My mind's going in all directions. Antoinette just died right here in my arms! All I could do was hold her; she couldn't speak, she was choking to death. Yeah, the nurse pronounced and left an hour ago. I don't want to talk about it now. Let's talk later, okay?"

I ended the phone call, rose from the chair and walked from the tiny kitchen into the living room, stopping next to her fallen body. Narrow rays of sunlight filtered through the window shade, hitting the floor, illuminating the palm of Antoinette's small wrinkled hand, the only part of her not quite covered by the faded blue sheet. Reaching down, I made adjustments so only the imprint of her body was displayed. Even with the atmospheric conditioner on, the apartment smelled stuffy.

Antoinette had lived in this tiny apartment for 40 years, never giving it or herself a makeover. Her impressive collection of antique dolls and figurines sat on shelves depicting a multitude of glass eyes mindlessly staring in all directions. The uniqueness of their design was diminished by the cloud of death that hung in the air. In the last six months, I had grown fond of her, and we developed a mutually respectful hospice patient, to hospice social worker relationship. We connected so fabulously because I was the son she wished for and she, the mother, I would have given my eyeteeth to have known.

Being a witness to 79-year-old Antoinette slowly succumbing to tongue cancer had been nerve-racking. To some, that may sound narrow-minded and selfish; however, that menacing mindset cropped up at every visit. Her swollen tongue partly protruded from both sides of her mouth, garbling her speech; however, after a few visits, conversations with her became second nature. We shared the realization that she would likely die from asphyxiation, and nothing short of assisted suicide or the removal of her tongue could alter that fate. Faithfully, she held onto the belief that she was headed to a better place than this world and pooh-poohed having regrets of any kind.

I arrived only hours ago, gave Antoinette a big hug and listened while she excitedly shared details of the latest mystery novel she had been reading. Suddenly and without warning, both of her pupils rolled up, leaving her eyes a ghostly white. Though stunned, I was eerily aware of my sudden impotence and watched in horror as she vainly attempted to force open her jaws. For a very brief moment, our eyes met, and we shared the realization that she had breathed her last bit of precious air. I let out a small cry, and immediately, tears welled up in my eyes. Through my tear-soaked gaze, her blurred image fell forward, and I reached out blindly, thanking God I was able to catch her full weight before she hit the floor.

I closed my eyes and held her until the convulsions subsided. I honestly don't know how long I sat slowly rocking her body from side to side. I wanted to cry, but dared not to; this was Antoinette's time. I needed this to be all about her. When my eyes opened, her face was a peaceful, splendid blue background to her grotesquely bloated tongue. I continued to sit for a few minutes, surveying all the stuff she spent her life collecting.

There was an ornate bone-white china set on the kitchen table, complete with white silk napkins, sterling silver forks, knives and spoons. I recalled Antoinette humorously saying, her home was always ready for guests that would never arrive. The obligatory call to her son lasted two minutes; his indifference to his mother's death was only overshadowed by his concern for her jewelry, doll collection and savings. She had spoken about many highlights of her life, but her son was noticeably not one of them.

My phone rang again, drawing me away from my memories of Antoinette's death. The name and number that flashed on the screen belonged to my co-worker Sara. My heart usually did a little dance while talking with her. I genuinely cared for her (my little secret), it was not unusual while I was in her company to fantasize about kissing her. She, in turn, felt comfortable sharing personal thoughts with me. We could talk for hours. At the present moment, I longed to be held in her embrace. Reluctantly, I put those feelings aside and answered the call.

"Hey, Nurse Sara, how're you doing?

"Don't give me that, I'm okay, greeting. I heard what happened. I want you to know that I'm proud of you for being there with Antoinette. Ever since she came on hospice, you showed up for her every week. So, how are you really doing?"

"I'm hanging in there."

"Jay, you know that I'm always here for you, right?"

Words failed me for a few taut moments, and my throat felt constricted as I let the words "I know" fall out of my mouth.

"It's going to be all right, Jay. I also called to let you know that I'm almost at the apartment of our new patient, Maria Garcia; you gonna meet me there?

"Soon as I can, waiting for the funeral guy to pick up Antoinette."

"She looked forward to your visits, you know."

"Yeah…I know." I wanted to change the subject, so I asked if she knew of any social issues with the new patient.

"Nah, seems routine, but who knows?"

The doorbell rang, and I nearly jumped out of my skin. I looked through the peephole and saw a guy in a suit and tie with a gurney in tow.

"Gotta go, Antoinette's ride is here; see you later."

"Okay, Jay."

I opened the door and asked if he was from Piazzo's Funeral Home. "Yeah, I'm Ralph, the transporter."

I fought the urge not to shake his hand; there was something about certain undertakers that left your hand feeling slimy. I guess undertakers grossed out most people. Dentists probably came in a close second. Ralph kept talking as he walked to the body, "Sorry I'm late. I was busy with a burial; the dead guy must've known half of the people in this city and then some." Ralph looked down at Antoinette and commented, "It's not like she was going anywhere, know what I'm saying?" I smiled to be polite silently wishing I could take my handshake back. I had to say it, "You know that's someone's mom?"

He stopped and looked me in the eyes; he must've seen something in them. He bit his lip, quickly looked away and said,

"Yeah, that's true, my bad."

I watched with apprehension as Ralph prepped Antoinette, to his credit; he handled her like the fine China she used to delicately dust. He pressed a lever, collapsing the gurney to the floor, slid a grey body bag under her and zippered it in one fell swoop without disturbing one strand of her thin white hair. Gently, he moved the body onto the gurney, keeping one hand on her legs while the gurney sprang up waist-high.

In an overly loud voice, he exclaimed, "Hey buddy, everything's done on my end, just need your John Hancock." After signing, I opened the door and watched Antoinette exiting her apartment for the last time. I had seen hundreds of people at the end of their lives, but, Antoinette's brand of courage and acceptance wowed me to the core. Even while she was dying, she constantly told me to never stop helping people. She said, "You have an innate ability to make a difference, a strong one, and I have been blessed to have you here with me."

I just thanked her, shook my head and smiled. I don't know if my presence made a difference when her moment came. Nevertheless, in the end, death is a solitary experience. I was really going to miss her. I turned off the atmospheric conditioner, closed the curtains, shut off the lights, stepped into the hallway and locked the door. According to her son's wishes, I left the key under the mat.

I walked leisurely down the ten flights of stairs to the lobby, stood behind the glass doors and watched people on the sidewalk stroll by. From where I stood, the passersby appeared to be silent travelers moving to and from their individual destinations. Some wore goggles, and all wore breathing masks of one kind or another, reminding me once again that decades of air pollution had significantly poisoned Earth's atmosphere. Forty years ago, it became a critical problem when 25% of newborns came into the world with respiratory issues. Even that wasn't enough to give the "powers that be" a major jolt. The Environmental Protection Agency made a knee-jerk response and passed a handful of minor regulations that resulted in the major polluters finding less noticeable ways to poison the earth.

It became a global geopolitical crisis event when decades of research studies revealed that the decrease in oxygen and increase in airborne toxins was the reason why 30% of all women were infertile. That bit of news caused religious leaders from all faiths to rain down fire and brimstone upon the President, Congress and the Senate. Faster than Moses parted the Red Sea, the United States Environmental Protection Agency along with the President's endorsement, initiated martial law mandating that all Americans were to wear personal respirators when outside of their atmospherically controlled residences.

Landlords had tried and failed to repeal the new law mandating them to buy and install "atmospheric air convertors" in all rental properties, but to no avail. Every building owner in America where people worked and lived was legally required to install the convertors, from the most expensive penthouses to the lowliest of hovels.

In the beginning of what came to be known as the "Fresh Air for America" initiative, the federal government ordered and paid for the production of mass quantities of personal respirators. In the beginning, they gave them out like government cheese. Private respirator companies shot up like wildfire. Eventually, it became too costly, and a "quickie" legislative law passed the buck to the states, who in turn passed it on to its citizens. The government's official posture for the respirator masks and fresh air convertors cited health risks and the prevention of human extinction as the overriding reason. Anyone with half a brain knew the laws were enacted to quell the clergy and keep costs down so that the super wealthy, who in fact, were largely responsible for the problem, were not financially burdened by this social disaster.

How much money a person was worth determined the quality of fresh air they breathed. When outside of their atmospherically controlled residences, the upper class wore a SCBA (self-contained breathing apparatus). In essence, they carried 12 hours of concentrated fresh air. The less fortunate wore PR masks (particulate respirator), which filtered out most (not all) of the toxic particles from the atmosphere. The dirt poor and street people wrapped a bandana around their faces and hoped for the best.

It reminded me of my childhood in Brooklyn. My mother, sister, and I sometimes wore PRs, and when money was scarce, we tied bandanas over our mouths and noses. Sometimes, my mother washed the bandanas twice a day. She did her best to make ends meet and keep us out of poverty. My dear old dad was nowhere to be found and existed as a faded picture tucked away somewhere and a bad taste in my mom's mouth. Growing up without a father figure was for me, and most likely for most, a distinct social and psychological disadvantage.

Most of the books in school focused on families with a mother and a father. The missing parent in my life left a void. I found my missing sense of self in music. I learned to play the guitar. I took lessons with an old Jewish music teacher who lived in my neighborhood. The guitar strings hurt my soft young fingers; nevertheless, I persisted and became very proficient.

I listened to the songs about hope and love. I strongly identified with the words expressed in the songs of the Beatles, jazz and blues artists. Show tunes offered culture and a historical perspective.

Hard rock and pop music kept me in tune with the ever-changing landscape of life. This eclectic mix (in my mind), brought me to a safe place, offering some answers to my questioning soul (answers that probably saved me from the many perils inherent with growing up "Black and poor" in America).

I took my SCBA from my bag, attached it securely to my face and walked out of the building. Once in my car, I removed the SCBA, adjusted the oxygen level in the car and drove to meet Sara. The potholes in the road rocked the car to the left, causing me to tighten my grip on the wheel and neatly swerve the car ever so slightly to the right to avoid straying into the opposing traffic lane.

The roads were lousy with potholes of formidable sizes; repairing them had become too expensive for most large cities. Times were hard, and the middle class were a small stratum of society. The larger portions of people were the working poor or the impoverished dregs of society. That left the elite and the social role I played, a small compressed stratum of the upper-middle class. As a rule, fewer cars were being manufactured. Gas-powered cars had become a novelty, replaced by less expensive and much cleaner solar-driven vehicles. Alas, it was too little too late for Earth's atmosphere.

I set the car radio to 1010 WINS, and just like their

slogan, "Don't leave home without it," I seldom did. Soon after I graduated from college, WINS and all the news media were reporting daily about a mysterious old age-related medical disorder. The media dubbed it the "Methuselah epidemic" after the man in the Hebrew Bible who had lived the longest. It seemed to only infect rich guys. White men of means were dying by the thousands from this unknown disease. It left the host body looking decades older than its real age.

In my capacity as a hospice social worker, I had personally seen hundreds of male patients succumb to this mysterious old age disorder. Why they chose hospice care was beyond me. Each of them could have bought their own nursing home. As a social scientist, it fascinated me, and though I tried to get more insight into the epidemic, to my vexation, by the time I saw them, not one of the "Methuselah" patients retained the ability to make intelligible speech. They usually expired within a few days. Even stranger, six months after the Methuselah patients began to show up, reports of child abductions dramatically increased.

Within the last few years, the abductions had rapidly

accelerated, people from all walks of life were disappearing. Now, it was a social problem of epic proportions, and New York City appeared to be at the epicenter. Most of the city lived in fear of rapidly aging and dying or being abducted, never to be seen again. There were forums, news reports, street protests, speeches from law enforcement and politicians, but nothing stopped the so-called Methuselah epidemic or the abductions. In the end, religious zealots and extremists from all faiths utilized the mass hysteria to progress their individual doctrines, declaring that the "end of days" were upon us.

I knew better than to buy into their warped theological rantings. There was a real-world explanation. Suddenly, in my peripheral vision, I saw a man jaywalking into my traffic lane. I slammed on the brakes and coaxed the sliding car to one side; I missed hitting him by a couple of feet. We eyeballed each other for a few seconds. A couple of passersby darted their eyes at the scene and continued on their way. The jaywalker was in his 20s, dressed in sneakers and shorts as if it was a warm day in July. He mumbled something under his SCBA, gave me the finger and slipped away.

I smiled and clicked on my dash computer to review the info on the new hospice patient. Her name was Maria Garcia, and her family personified the classic god-fearing, culturally close-knit, co-dependent and emotionally charged Hispanic family that bore watching. Ten years as a hospice clinician taught me to be prepared when dealing with the impending death of the matriarch of a traditional Hispanic family. There was the potential for lots of drama. I put the car in gear and continued on to the apartment of the

Garcia family; they lived in the public housing projects on West 125th street.

The skyline of the city whizzed by, and affluent high-rise buildings were steadily replaced by low-rise tenements, condemned buildings and street people wearing a veil of overwhelming despair. It made me think of my roots. Growing up, my family lived as if interacting with each other was a hideous social disease to be avoided at all costs. My childhood was interwoven with family secrets, saturated with alcoholic uncles, sprinkled with lies and domestic violence.

As a means of self-preservation, I passionately studied

Tae Kwon Do Karate, earning a third-degree black belt, a natural response to the violence I witnessed at home. Another part of it was about protecting myself from a violent world in which I felt very alone. Despite it all, I had turned out all right. I had my back story, but, who didn't? Hey, I learned to love myself and, ultimately, others. It was a good trait to possess when working with people facing the end of their lives.

My intrapersonal moment was interrupted by the 1010 news announcer. I listened with a sense of foreboding as the announcer described how two crowds numbering in the hundreds, each representing radically different religious dogma, had converged at 34th Street and 6th Avenue. Both groups were carrying handmade signs warning the public to "repent," "God is coming," or to "Prepare for hell." Tempers were high when police in riot gear responded; several shots were fired from someone in the crowd, killing one cop and wounding four others, resulting in a stampede which trampled several children who were in serious but stable condition."

I slid the car into a tight space between a Ford van and a green Mercedes sedan, leaned back into the headrest and released a long, uneasy sigh. The world was going to hell in a basket, but I had to press on. I donned my SCBA, grabbed my shoulder bag and stepped out of the car. I took a few seconds to take in the dismal landscape of the public housing complex. I walked past several people wearing what amounted to dirty rags tied around their nose and mouth. Times like these made me feel guilty of being privileged to have a SCBA.

I made sure my I.D. card was visible. I wanted to avoid being robbed of my SCBA; they fetched a nice price in the underground market even though they contained tracking chips and drew long prison sentences for anyone caught stealing them. When I removed my SCBA in the building's lobby I was disappointed at the hint of foulness in the air. This usually was a sign that the atmospheric converter in the apartment building was of poor quality or in need of maintenance.

One of the pitfalls of visiting patients in their homes was not being able to wear a mask. It interfered with communicating and the building of trust. Masks were worn in the home only in extreme conditions. As I exited the elevator, the sound of my footsteps echoed down the stone-walled hallway, slowly abating when I stopped at apartment 6G. I rang the buzzer, wondering what was happening on the other side.

I smiled when the door opened, shook hands and introduced myself to Emma, the patient's daughter. She appeared to be 60ish, frail in stature and tired in a way that crept into the folds of her soul. Her smile was friendly as she ushered me into the small apartment chock full of sons, daughters, grandchildren, uncles, aunts, cousins, siblings and neighbors all dressed or speaking in somber tones.

Emma was easy to engage as she talked about changing countless adult diapers for her mother, Maria. She often wondered if she ever became bedbound and incontinent, would her own children be as committed to her personal care. She explained how frustrated she was after deciding to quit her job of 15 years after her "family leave" ran out. She was too young for social security and dependent upon the part-time income of an alcoholic husband when he was able to show up for work. Her mother Maria had been a factory worker, and $497.00 in monthly social security benefits was the financial sum total of her mother's life's work.

We walked toward the rear of the apartment and headed to what I assumed to be the bedroom of the patient, I spied Sara with her hands buried in her nursing bag, and before I could speak, she spun around with a big grin, saying, "Hey sweetie, how's it going?" Sara's easy-going, savoir-faire attitude reminded me that she was one of those rare people pre-destined to become a nurse or someone who let people know that they were not alone in their feelings of being overwhelmed by it all.

"I'm fine Sara, and you're looking good." She laughed and telegraphed her trademark wink at me as we followed Emma deeper into the confines of the apartment. Sara grabbed my arm to slow me down, I leaned toward her, and she whispered, "One of my daughter's friends disappeared on her way home from school three days ago. She was only six years old, Jay…I think it's related to this Methuselah epidemic. Jay, I can't watch Laura every hour of the day. If anything happens to her, I don't know what I'd do." All I could manage was a quick touch of her shoulder and a nod of my head as we entered the room.

We stepped into a colorfully decorated bedroom;

wallpapered with family pictures and lots of flowers, both real and artificial. The children played while the adults talked in small groups. Sara and I smiled at every pair of eyes that met ours. In the farthest corner of the room, Maria, the dying matriarch, was fully alert and lay bedbound with lethargic splendor. Before I could utter a word, she met my gaze and said quite loudly,

"Buenos Dias Senor?"

"Buenos Días Señora como está usted?"

"Muy bien gracias y usted." "Bien gracias"

Those few words caused her to breathe very rapidly and kicked up a racking cough loud enough to be heard throughout the apartment. Emma moved quickly, brought a cup of water to Maria's lips while a few of the older women made the sign of the cross. Maria wasn't quite ready to meet her maker, she recovered, and the sparkle in her eyes returned. Her eyes and skin were a yellowish tint. The cancer had begun to metastasize to her liver and kidneys, and at best, she had a few months to live. Emma began to describe how good God had been in their lives ever since they ran away from the Castro regime in Cuba over 500 years ago (ancient history).

Emma's body suddenly stiffened as she explained the fear Cubans experienced back then, from President Alejandro Castro Ruz, to the fear of being kidnapped or dying of accelerated old age. It took me a moment to realize she was referring to the street abductions and the Methuselah epidemic. She went on to explain that these were the kinds of thoughts shared by everyone she knew.

Suddenly, a chorus of loud screams and gasps drew my attention. The sounds were coming from the living room, reflexively all of us turned toward the commotion and witnessed, Roberto, Emma's very drunk and naked husband, stumbling into the room, angrily shouting, "Las personas diablo! No seta Muertos!" After a few more threatening insults, Roberto made a clumsy move towards Sara. It was clear that he resented the presence of hospice.

Before I could respond, Emma had calmly risen from her seat, picked up speed and slammed her small body into her portly husband, screaming, "No Bruto, No Hoy!" Everyone within eyesight and earshot moaned in disbelief. Roberto crumbled to the floor like a bad joke, and Emma, with one of her hands firmly in his armpit; the other, tightly grasping his wrist, dragged him into a back room.

She slammed the door so hard the entire apartment trembled.

Emma regained her composure no differently than a matador who had suffered injury; however, she had still slayed thc bull. She returned and continued to share stories of her mother and deceased father. She was proud of her dad, a renowned Quattro guitarist, and though he had fathered more children than Emma had fingers and toes; she carried a torch for him that blazed ferociously in her eyes as she told stories of this very gifted artist.

After a while, she rose, excused herself and left the room. She returned excited, tenderly holding the most magnificent guitar I had ever seen. I instinctively reached out my hands, saying, "May I?" With a quizzical smile, she said, "By all means."

I tuned the strings and carefully fingered the opening chords to "Don't Cry for Me Argentina," the mood in the apartment shifted and moved from simmering coals to a fiery wave of hope and passion. There was no need to sing the words; the guitar was saying it all. Each note found its mark. Every person in the tiny apartment was drawn in like moths to a flame. The radiant sounds brought a momentary cessation of their grief. Not long after, Sara and I said our goodbyes. Emma followed us into the hallway.

"What do I do if my mother dies? Do I call your agency or the hospital?"

In a very caring tone, Sara replied, "Call our agency, and a nurse will be sent to do the pronouncement." She stressed, "Don't call 911." Emma nodded slowly in agreement apparently trying not to picture that experience.

This was my opening, "Emma, have you and your mother discussed what her wishes are when she passes? Did she tell you what she desired for funeral plans?"

"Oh yes, my mother is very religious and always plans ahead. She even picked out the dress and shoes she wanted to be buried in and the songs to be played at her service. My older brother Marcos is handling all the details."

We chatted with Emma for a few minutes, then took turns hugging. She watched us walk to the elevator. Once downstairs, we donned our SCBAs and stepped out into the street, and that's when Sara gripped my elbow with both hands.

"Jay"?

"Yeah?"

"You know how sometimes we share personal stuff?" "Uh huh, is this one of those times?"

"Yeah, this is one of those times."

The rawness of her vulnerability filled my senses. Whatever it was, it was very important to her.

"There's a diner down the block; let's go; I could eat a little something." "Thanks, I really appreciate this."

"No problem; I'm going to need to dump some things on you soon." She smiled and said affectionately, "I'm ready when you are."

After our waitress had seated us, I looked up from stirring my coffee, waiting for Sara to speak. She sat across the table, trying not to look directly at me. She was obviously nervous. Her dark brown hair was parted in the middle, and a flawless braid peeked over her shoulder. I toyed with the idea of gently moving it so that it peeked over her other shoulder. I resisted the temptation. The waitress returned to the table, took our orders and disappeared behind the swinging doors that led to the noisy kitchen. Sara leaned forward, bringing her face closer to mine. I could see tears in the corner of her eyes and felt her uneasiness as she spoke.

"I feel…I need to get it out." Her eyes were wide open, and her mouth quivered as she searched for the words. Her body rocked slowly, not unlike the furrows of angry waves on the incoming tide. I sat still, anticipating her flood of words. She did not disappoint me.

"That scene between Emma and her husband kicked up some bad emotions in me. She stared through me for a few long seconds, then spoke trancelike.

"When I was 17, I got pregnant from Tom, my daughter's father. I lived at home with my parents, When they found out, they were devastated. We got married quickly, and I moved in with Tom. He always told me he would take care of me. I had no reason not to trust him."

She took a long breath, and my eyes settled onto the creases on her beautiful face. Her voice began to waver, and I became all ears.

"Things were okay until my daughter Laura was born, then things began to change. She whispered so low I had to lean forward to hear, "It started with small things, you know, a negative comment about my body or how I sucked at sex. I'll never forget the day he called me a stupid bitch." Sara saw the waitress walking towards our table and stopped talking. After our orders were placed on the table and the waitress was gone, she picked up the conversation.

"I didn't say anything; I didn't want Laura to see us arguing. The cursing got worse. One day, I told him that I had to start helping my father take care of my mother. She was home from the hospital bedbound and partially paralyzed from a recent stroke. That son of a bitch blocked the door and wouldn't let me and Laura leave. The next day, I waited for him to go to work, and Laura and I went to help my mother."

"We got home an hour before he usually got in, and he was sitting in the living room waiting. I…" she pauses, "felt something hot on my leg and realized I peed my pants! I stood there, scared-stiff, and waited. I waited for him to drink his beer, and he told me to put Laura to bed. The moment I returned to the living room, he backhanded my face, and I laid crying on the floor while his foot fractured two of my ribs."

She began to cry uncontrollably, with both hands covering her face. The waitress had been approaching the table, stopped, took in the scene, looked accusingly at me and made a U-turn. A couple at another table threw side glances in our direction, trying not to be obvious. I got up and sat beside her with my arm around her shoulders; she rested her head on my arm. My intention was to comfort her; however, the pleasure I derived from her leaning body upon mine, I shamelessly enjoyed.

"You don't have to tell me anymore, okay?" We were both quiet for about a minute, and in a resolute tone, she continued.

"He apologized every day for a month; bought me flowers, and gave me permission to help my mother. I told everyone I had fallen down the stairs. When my injuries almost healed, I got Laura ready, and we went to help my father care for my mother. Things got a little better for a while, and then the verbal abuse started again, along with hard slaps to my ass."

"When I began to ignore the slaps and talked back to him, he began to rape me. It didn't matter whether Laura was in the living room watching television. He would grab me by my wrist, pull me into the bedroom, slam the door and rip my clothes off." She started to shake; I held her closer, wishing I could have been there to save her. Sara took another deep breath, then spoke.

"One evening, as I was planning to leave my parents' home, Laura complained of a stomach and headache. Her temperature was 102 degrees. My parents insisted that I stay and not take Laura out into the frigid air. I gave her children's aspirin and put her to bed. I was scared. I had never spent the night out since I was married. I called Tom's number and felt a rush of relief when it went to his voicemail. I explained Laura's condition and told him we'd be home tomorrow evening after I finished taking care of my mother." "I didn't sleep; I rocked Laura to sleep and continued to rock for the rest of the night. When we returned home the next evening, the lights in our first-floor apartment were out, and the door was partly open. I stuck my head in and called out Tom's name. I was met by a fist that instantly broke my nose; Tom dragged me into the apartment while Laura held frantically onto my leg. The door slammed shut, and I blacked out."

"When I regained consciousness, Laura was screaming "no daddy, no… bad daddy, don't hurt mommy!" Blood flowed from my nose, into my mouth and down my neck. My words floundered like someone drowning under water. His hands wrapped around my throat and his eyes gleamed down at me. Through the horror I could vaguely hear him shouting.

"You bitch, you don't sleep out unless I say it's all right, I'm the man. You got it? I'M THE MAN!"

"I had no fight left in me. My eyes were close to bursting out of my sockets when I looked up; I saw the image of my father's angry face standing over Tom's head; I thought I was hallucinating. I heard a thumping sound, looked and saw Tom's bloodied head lying beside me. His eyes were fused shut. It was surreal, I was thinking that it had been a long time since I felt no fear of him, and at that moment, I felt none, absolutely none. Part of me wished that he was dead and would never wake up."

"I looked up, and my father was bending down towards me with a bloody set of brass knuckles on his hand. At first, I said it softly, you knew, you knew, and then I screamed— you knew it all the time! I cried longer than I have ever cried in my life. From the kitchen, I heard music; the radio was playing the song "Night Train" by Soul Asylum. Do you know that one?"

I nodded yes. As Sara continued to talk, I stared into her eyes while, in my head listened to the lyrics to that song—

Runaway train never going back, wrong way on a one-way track. Seems like I should be getting somewhere; somehow, I'm neither here, nor there.

"My daughter and I spent a week at my parents and a year at a domestic violence safe house. By the second month at the shelter, I divorced Tom. My mother died during the sixth month, and three months later, my father followed her. My parents were kindred spirits and I knew as much as he loved me and Laura, he could not wait to join my mother." I smiled at Sara, she smiled back, and we stared at each other for a few seconds.

"You must think I'm such a big crybaby?"

"Of course I don't. It makes me feel good that you wanted to share this with me."

She wiped her eyes, and a big smile formed on her lips.

"Well, after all, you are my office husband."

We laughed as I walked Sara to her car. We had hugged before, but this time, I realized I really cared for her and very soon would need to let her know how I felt. I wondered what the outcome of that conversation would be. I purposely dismissed those thoughts from my mind and drove to Bedford-Stuyvesant, Brooklyn.

Driving through my old neighborhood ignited some of my thoughts and memories. Ever since I could remember, my family's unwritten code was essentially, not to tell each other the truth. I could still see the alcoholic uncles, hear the lies and feel the violence my mother endured from her relationships with men. I easily identified with Sara. Personal traumas have a way of showing up when you least expect them to.

All that drama actually helped me to become a very good clinician and professor. I was grateful to have the ability to identify with people struggling to restore a semblance of normalcy to their lives. Going through hard times was part of life. The turning point in my life rested heavily on my decision not to emulate my family but to view them as bad examples to be avoided, as if they were cancerous.

I continued driving down Fulton Street; there was a lot of activity in the streets, especially around the Muslim temples, Jewish synagogues and the Baptist churches. The people milled around, some looked angry, and others huddled together with worried looks, carrying signs warning about the "Methuselah" plague and people being kidnapped by the government for experimental purposes.

Things seemed primed for an all-out riot. I didn't have long to puzzle over that possibility before I arrived at the grossly neglected four-family home where Tanisha lived. I entered the unlocked front door and knocked on the first-floor apartment on the left. While I waited, I scanned the dark hallway with its large patches of decades-old peeling paint.

After several minutes I could hear several door locks being opened to reveal my patient Tanisha. She was a single 32-year-old African-American female with an especially aggressive form of brain cancer. She elected to be placed on hospice once all life-sustaining measures had been exhausted. This was our sixth monthly home visit.

She smelled of urine, undaunted; I hugged her just like

I always did. She excused herself and slowly, painfully, ambled to the bathroom.

I watched her, quietly struggle across the room; she winced in pain through every step of her ordeal. I saw a glimpse of triumph cover her face once her hand touched the knob to the bathroom door. Both of us knew that one fall would result in a lonely death in a hospital. But she was adamant about not using diapers or a bedside commode. When the bathroom door opened, I didn't look in her direction until, Tanisha was standing beside me.

"So, what's my social worker thinking about?"

"Well, since you ask, I want to make sure you're comfortable and safe, and I'm wondering what you need done around here?

She placed her hand on the side of her head while squinting her eyes. I wasn't sure if she was feeling pain or in deep thought. Finally, she spoke.

"Yeah, my driver's license expired. I never let that happen."

There was no chance in hell that she would ever drive

again, but people facing imminent death require hope. We began to look for the personal documents needed to reinstate her license. In our search, my eyes came fully into view of her bald head. It bore the lurid scars of unsuccessful surgeries and was the causality of her wobbly gait. All of this reminded me why I continued to work with hospice patients.

"Jay, I have to use the ladies room again."

I simply smiled as she began her slow trek to the bathroom. I took the time to allow reflection to take over my thoughts—

Occasionally, the faces of some of the deceased patients visited me, and I survived the resultant emotions by remembering the good that came out of each experience. At times, the burden of being the one delegated to help ease the strife caused by the dying process became overwhelming. My way of reducing stress was to work out at the gym. This amounted to running on the treadmill, using weight machines to increase strength or doing laps in the pool at the university. I was an athlete in college, a long-distance runner and swimmer and personally, it was important for me to stay in shape.

Music and movies were also avenues of retreat. I loved to escape into the dark confines of a movie theatre. When I entered the theatre, I felt transported as if Scotty from the ancient Star Trek Enterprise movies had engineered my release by beaming me to a blissful place. I loved hearing the voice of a woman coming from the ticket-vending robot (live people in movie theatres were a thing of the past). The voice said, "Which movie and how many tickets?"

I looked to my left, then to my right, smiled and said, "Just one" to the vending robot, who collected my plastic money and gave me a ticket to enter the lobby of the theatre. After entering the lobby and proceeding to the refreshment counter, where I ordered a medium popcorn and drink from a mechanical counter person. The next few hours were mine completely, my cocoon far away from reality.

Music had evolved into digital pulses that created sounds. Even the vocals were man-made. Recorded music with live singers was rare, though there were still private collectors. Music of live events or concerts existed in very few collections, most of these were on display at museums or could be viewed in special libraries. People who actually played instruments, such as myself, were a dying breed.

There had been a war every ten years in which whole cities had been decimated. Countries still fought hand-to-hand combat against each other; however, it usually ended with the flip of a switch, which ignited a storm of missiles, killing thousands. The United States, Russia, China, Japan, France, England and Germany had never had a military attack from another country. Terrorist organizations kill hundreds every year in all of the aforementioned countries. Less than two months ago, a well-coordinated attack in Washington, D.C. destroyed the west wing of the white house, killing six members of the President's staff. A known Ukrainian terrorist group took credit for the bombing.

An interesting article posted on the Internet from the New York Times pointed out that the presidential staff was replaced within 12 hours. Prestige won over risk in that recruitment process.

Kubler Ross is considered to be the guru on death and dying, and she asserted, "Groups of people, from street gangs to nations, may use their group identity to express their fear of being destroyed by attacking and destroying others. Is war perhaps nothing else but a need to face death, to conquer and master it, to come out of it alive, a peculiar form of denial of our own mortality?"

"If all of us would make an all-out effort to contemplate our own death, to deal with our anxieties surrounding the concept of our own death, it would be interesting to see if this would make a difference in our aggression towards each other."

—Tanisha's coughing brought me back from my reflections. She had returned and did so ever so silently.

"You know, I've been on my own since I was 15. My parents dropped me off at school, and I never saw them again. My teacher and the principal told me that they burned to death in a car accident, I cried a lot, and sometimes I still do."

I listened—

"I moved in with my aunt, quit school in the tenth grade and got a job as a nanny. I had a fake I.D. and told families I was 18; I've always been a big girl and looked older. She took a stab at sitting down, missed the chair, causing me to lurch forward and guide her onto the sofa.

She closed her eyes, formed a smile and turned to me.

"This was my first apartment, this is my home, I'm gonna die here, you know?"

I looked into her eyes, which were now open. "Yeah… I know."

We found her documents and completed her license renewal. I stayed another hour listening to her life review. Tanisha openly shared her successes and dreams. Ever since my first visit, I had never heard her complain once about any part of her experiences. She blamed no one and always looked at her positives. Finally, we hugged again, and I went home. I had the sinking feeling that I would not see her again. I didn't sleep well that night. It was the shrill ring of my cell phone that woke me early the next morning. I rolled over to answer it even though tiredness told me to let it go to voicemail.

"Hello"

"Jay? Hey man, its Rick, Rick Brown. I know it's kind of early —how's it going, buddy?"

Rick Brown and I went way back, knew him since our freshman year in high school. He was on the football team and I ran track and was on the swimming team. We lived one block from each other and our personalities were as different as night and day. He looked at the world soundly grounded to the earth and I had my head in the clouds.

He lived with both parents. As a teenager, Rick's life, morals and values were strongly influenced by religion. He spent quite a bit of his time in church. His girlfriend was a "church girl," and they practiced celibacy. I, on the other hand, was a latchkey kid with a very liberal mother who had never stopped playing the field. After losing my virginity at age 17, having sex with girls was an expected part of my existence.

My family's values and morals were all over the place, the few that I could remember. I'll never forget that summer when I was seventeen. A very pretty and well-developed girl moved into our Brooklyn neighborhood. She was doing everything possible to get my attention. Both Rick and I were enamored by her sweet, southern charm. I began to buckle, disregarding my "larger head" for my "smaller" one.

One day, after I had convinced myself to "do the deed" with her, Rick pulled me aside and very adamantly told me something we both knew, and I chose to ignore. The girl looked sixteen, but, was only thirteen. Despite my strong will and lack of parental guidance, I listened to him and backed off. In hindsight, I was thankful that someone took the time to try and set me straight.

Regardless of our personal differences, we respected each other and remained best friends until we lost contact during our college years. We reconnected several years ago and I ended up being the best man at his wedding. His wife was a beautiful woman, and Rick's kids called me Uncle Jay. They were the closest thing I had to a family.

"Hey Rick, I'm doing okay; it's good to hear from you; too long, it's been…"

"A long time, my friend; you're right, too long."

"Yeah, sounds like you've got something on your mind?" "That's why we call you "Mr. Analysis."

"So, Mr. Comedian… What can I do you for?"

"I'm calling, about this Methuselah epidemic, at least that's what the media is calling it."

"What about it, Rick? You know something the rest of us don't?"

"Not really; I was assigned to examine the bodies of the last 15 victims. So far, I've come up with zilch, nothing that explains this rapid aging phenomenon."

"So…the Assistant Chief Pathologist for the City of New York is calling a little-known social work professor and hospice clinician for his professional opinion? Hmmm…. let me check my fee schedule."

"All right, Professor, I'm sure I can talk my wife into inviting you over for dinner whenever it's convenient for you."

"A home-cooked meal? Say no more; you've got a deal!"

We talked for over two hours. I was glad for the opportunity to become involved, really involved in this mysterious epidemic. I asked him question after question from the beginning to the end about what he knew or suspected. One thing we agreed on was that the unknown agent had to be inorganic. Something man-made was causing the accelerated aging.

At the end of our conversation, I suggested that the unknown agent could have been artificially introduced into the body and that since a blood-borne passageway had been ruled out, the next most likely source would be the spinal fluid to which Rick happily replied,

"Now, that's really why we call you Mr. Analysis. Of course, that's the next best way to effectively affect the brain and organs. The spinal fluid, who would've thought? All kidding aside, this could be a real breakthrough. I can't wait to run the tests and get back to you. Talk to you soon, my friend and thanks, I mean that. The kids send their love."

"Hey Rick, what about our… deal?" Too late, he was gone.

I lay in bed staring at the sunlight streaming in through the window shades, creating rows of light on the wall. My mind was overwhelmed with questions about the Methuselah patients. Eventually, I lapsed into an uneasy sleep. I dreamed I was walking down a narrow, dark path, aware of something, searching and seeking to do me harm. This went on for what seemed hours until I spread my arms into a six-foot wingspan, lifting me off the ground, high into the air and far above the treacherous path. I woke feeling a strong sense of uncertainty.

Chapter II: Just Another Day In Hospice

My body has grown weaker many years, the days are long, yet still, I have not time. I must prepare.

A woman learns a lot, if she survives - and may you learn from this, my death, the knowledge gained to my last breath. The men, the professors, cannot know what rigors I persisted in to find the secrets of the atom; but my mind is clouded as my sight, and now I go.

My child, I am proud of you it grieves me now to quit my life - adieu. Paraphrased from Marie Curie (1867-1934).

My first patient of the day was new to me; her name was Linda Lonegan.

She lived with her son Phillip on the 43rd floor of an

Upper East Side apartment building. It was overcast when I left the small studio I rented in Brooklyn. I drove mechanically to Manhattan, vaguely remembering passing over the Brooklyn Bridge. I removed my SCBA in the lobby of the Lonegan building and stood for a moment, closed my eyes and took in the freshness of the air. Funny, I couldn't remember the last time I breathed in such quality air.

Minutes later, I was engaged in conversation with Phillip, who sat across from me in his very luxurious living room. There was no denying his blunt and cavalier demeanor. His no-nonsense approach was for all intents and purposes, compelling.

"I never thought I'd have to put my finger up my mother's ass; I mean, what son thinks he'd have to care for his dying mother and use his finger to dis-impact her so she could get some relief?" Phillip Lonegan's face was bright and alive as he explained to me the daily challenges of caring for his mom. He was an only child, and it was evident that he loved and worshipped her.

"I'm a lot older than you; I grew up in a time when family took care of family. There was no depending on others to do what you didn't feel like doing. I had to work my ass off in law school. My family wasn't as well off as the other students. I had to pay for most of my courses and wear my father's suits when a suit was required. He was almost 2 sizes larger than me, and the first time anyone tried to make me into a joke, I took care of them in short order, yes I did."

"When I finished law school, I worked 25 years for the federal government. I stayed in private practice and retired three years ago when my wife was diagnosed with cancer. We had planned to travel the world and settle down on the island of Aruba, to live out the rest of our lives. I spent every single day with her for two years, and when she took her last breath in my arms, I held her for over an hour and then for another 20 minutes when the man from the funeral home arrived."

I silently wondered if it was Ralph, the transporter.

"He laid a green colored zippered body bag on one side of the bed and I insisted that I be allowed to place her into the bag. After managing that, I looked at her for a full five minutes; I only stopped because the funeral guy was starting to get restless. I slowly zippered the bag, lifted it onto the gurney and called my driver so that I could follow the hearse to the funeral home."

"A few days later, at her funeral, the Pastor was doing the sermon and at one point said, 'She was in a better place.' I stood up and shouted, "Are you fucking kidding me, she belongs with me! You know what's funny? There must've been 50 people in the room, and not one of them looked at me, not even the Pastor. They all got busy looking at their shoes or something. I sat down and didn't say another word through the sermon or at the cemetery."

"Three weeks ago, Linda, my 95-year-old mother, suffered a stroke; it left her unable to speak, completely paralyzed on her left side and oxygen dependent. Her body may be compromised, but her mind is sharp, piss-in-your-pants funny. She communicates by writing on a dry eraser board. You're a therapist; can I ask you a question?"

"Sure."

"After the hospital, I moved my mother here so I could take care of her; I wasn't going to let her die in a nursing home."

I waited for the question.

"Since she moved in, I know I should be sad that she's dying, but instead, I'm happy that I have someone to care for again. Do you think that's egotistical and self-centered?"

"I don't know, what do you think?" "I love her."

"So why don't we go with that?" "Yeah, I can live with that, thanks Jay."

"You're welcome, Phillip."

Phillip's cell phone began ringing, and whoever was on the other end caused him to stand up abruptly. He quickly excused himself and used his free hand to point me in the direction of what I presumed to be Linda's room. Then he literally sprinted into an outer room. I didn't expect such speed from such a large elderly man. I approached Linda's room and saw the door was slightly ajar.

I knocked, waited a few beats, and then stepped into the spacious, expensively decorated bedroom. Linda was in bed fully awake, and when we made eye contact, she beckoned me to come closer; she was a petite woman with shoulder-length salt and pepper hair. Her skin barely showed a wrinkle, and one had to look hard to see the very fine lines embedded in her face.

She met my smile, and I headed to the chair nearest her bed; she responded by patting the side of her bed and inviting me to sit there. I sat where she indicated. "Hello, Mrs. Lonegan, my name is" — she slowly extended her open palm, directing me to stop talking, and then she immediately began to write on her board. She wrote quickly and clearly and put the board in my hands. It said, "Nice to meet you, Jay and I know what you do and where you are from; I'm the boss around here, although my son may tell you differently. I wanted you to sit on my bed because I can't remember the last time a handsome stranger came to visit me!" She managed a clever half-smile.

I couldn't help laughing out loud. Her tiny frame shook as she attempted to voice her own laugh. She wrote, and I responded verbally for over an hour. Despite her formidable challenges, I marveled that she maintained a cool composure and an alluring wit. When the conversation shifted towards the end of life, she handed me the board; it said the following:

"Three women die in a car crash and go to heaven for

an orientation. They are all asked, when you're in your casket, what would you like to hear people say about you? The first woman says, I would like to hear them say that I was a great educator of my time and helped to teach many students. The second woman says, I would like to hear that I was a wonderful wife and loved by my husband and children. The last woman replies, I would like to hear them say, LOOK, SHE'S MOVING, SHE AIN'T DEAD!"

I could not remember the last time I laughed so hard and long. It made me want to pee so I excused myself to go to the restroom.

The apartment was cavernous; I counted at least five bedrooms and finally located a small room with an adjoining bathroom. While unbuckling my belt, I heard muffled voices in the adjacent room. The conversation sounded frantic and anxious; like the good social worker I was, I put my ear to the wall. It was Phillip talking loudly to another man.

"So, who do I have to blow to get some information? It's obvious I'm wasting my money on you. This thing is breaking out all over the country. What's that… the

Methuselah, for Christ's sake, where the hell have you been all these months, living in a cave?"

I knew that I was listening to a private conversation in a private residence, but once he mentioned the word *Methuselah*, I was all in; screw confidentiality and ethics. I could distinguish that the other person on the phone was on speaker, was a man and had a strong Hispanic accent.

"Phil, we need to meet soon, no more calls. How do you say? Oh yeah, we need a face-to-face. Everyone I speak to is scared; they don't want to say anything, not even for money. Maybe you should leave this one alone, huh?" "Marcos, we'll meet soon, but, if this goes as deep as you say, I need to make some moves now. We need more answers; right now, we're pissing in the wind, my friend."

The conversation sounded as if it was over, and I had some pissing of my own to do. Once done, I made my way back to Linda's room, and we resumed our conversation. Shortly after, Phillip entered the room, winked at me and asked if I would like a refreshment to which I replied, "No thank you," then continued reading Linda's message.

"I was blessed for over 50 years with the love of the most wonderful man ever created, and we brought into the world my son, who is my rock. I set things straight with all of my family and friends years ago so that we could all die in relative peace. I've never been religious; I am spiritual and ready for whatever comes after my life here ends." She reached for my hand, held it tightly and placed a small folded sheet of paper in the palm of my hand. It said, "Whenever you come to see me or whenever you think about me while I am alive or dead, remember that I was prepared for death and found the meaning of my life."

At each visit, those words she wrote, rang in my ears. My visits with Linda found her consistently open and responsive. Some visits lasted two hours, some longer. As her health declined, she began to write about her concerns for Phillip; she hinted he wasn't really who he pretended to be. I wasn't quite sure of what she meant by that, and when I pressed her for clarity, her eyes became fearful, so I backed off. Soon after, she lost the ability to write, which was a major challenge to our communication. I began to read her lips, facial expressions and hand gestures.

I also learned to tap into her silence. One theme was always present in our conversations, and it involved her anxiety surrounding Phillip's real line of work and the fear that he was in some sort of danger. On several visits, I was able to catch parts of Phillip's conversations, but it appeared that he was being more cautious.

Two months passed; in hospice two months can be a relatively long time. I continued to see Maria Rodriguez and her daughter Emma every week. When Maria lapsed into a coma, her daughter took her off of hospice so that she could receive life-sustaining treatment (a respirator). I came by every now and then to provide emotional support. Most of the time, Emma was giving he mother bed baths, repositioning her body and keeping her lips moist.

A total of six patients expired before I could get to see them. I had to find resources to bury three of them, and the other three needed food on the table and help paying their rent. Also, within those two months, Tanisha passed away. Her home health aide found her dead, lying on the floor halfway between her bed and the bathroom. The aide was very adamant about describing the smile Tanisha had on her face, even in death. I attended Tanisha's funeral at a small church in Bedford Stuyvesant, which was packed to the walls with mourners. She looked beautiful and happy lying in her white coffin. During the service, the Pastor asked if anyone wanted to come up to the microphone and say a few words about Tanisha. I'd spoken at quite a few funerals, and though I knew what I wanted to say when I reached the microphone, I became very emotional, and after speaking for 30 seconds, I began to cry so hard that returning to my seat became my only option.

That same evening, I received a call from Phillip Lonegan. "Hi Jay, I'm sorry to disturb you."

"Hey Phil, it's good to hear from you."

The sadness in his tone caused me to sit up. "What's on your mind?"

"I checked on my mother, and her lips were pursed in a sweet smile; when I pulled the covers up to keep her warm, my hand touched her face, and I pulled my hand back because her face was ice cold. It was then that I knew she was gone."

He paused, "Funny, there was no one else to call but

you. I don't mean that in a bad way. There was no one left that really mattered, but hospice. I'm going to sit here with her. Please send somebody; I'll just sit here and wait. Thanks for everything; in the short time that you were with us, you made a huge difference. She used to tell me every day."

Before I could respond, I realized he had hung up.

Linda was cremated according to her wishes, and a service was held a week later at a local church. Phillip insisted Sara, and I attend the funeral and sit in the first pew with him. It was a small affair, no more than 20 or 25 people. After the service, half of the attendees drove to the east river and as per Linda's wishes, her ashes were scattered into the wind, and we watched them float down into the dark waters. They took turns hugging Phillip, until only he, Sara and I were left. He seemed to be in a good place until his phone rang, and I could hear the man with the Hispanic accent. Phil gave us a quick hug and walked away with a pensive look on his face.

My cell phone rang as we approached our cars and the name on the caller I.D. made my heart skip a beat. I winked at Sara, leaned to kiss her cheek until I realized I was wearing my SCBA; instead, I hugged her and gestured that I needed to take the call. Walking away, I noticed she stood in the same spot, staring at me; a quizzical look framed her face.

Meanwhile, I was listening to the voice of Rick Brown, trying to make sense of his excitement.

"I tested and retested spinal fluid from all fifteen men who died from this old age disorder or *Methuselah* epidemic or whatever you want to call it. Fourteen came back clean. I got a positive indication of infection in the fifteenth one. I'm not a microbiologist, so I sent that specimen out to a lab outfitted to specify the strain."

"And what were the results? What did you find?"

I sat down on a nearby bench and checked the oxygen level on my SCBA. It had two hours of air left, and the local oxygen refilling station was only a few blocks away.

"It doesn't make sense; the lab found evidence of bacterial meningitis." "Meningitis, a brain infection?"

"Yeah, brain, spinal cord, and it's bacterial, so it's highly infectious. The point is, this guy was never diagnosed with meningitis. He never had symptoms, which is impossible because telltale signs were all over his nervous system and looked to be several years old. If that isn't weird enough, it's gone, Jay, just like he never had it. Somehow, the meningitis disappeared!"

"Give me some social history on the dead guy."

"Well, he didn't completely fit the *Methuselah* profile. He had the old age disorder, but it was not as advanced as the other bodies."

"Was he on hospice?"

"Wait a minute, I've got to check the file…"

I had a theory and needed more info from Rick.

"Let's see… uh, no he was found dead at home by his housekeeper."

"You know, you're suggesting that someone or something removed the meningitis out of this guy's body?"

"Yeah, that's what it looks like so far. Another thing, I sent my preliminary reports to my director, and the responses I'm getting from the higher-ups are making me nervous. I don't feel comfortable talking about this on the phone, and I need to follow up on some more things. Let's make plans to touch base in a few days."

We ended the call on that ominous note. That evening, I was scheduled to teach at the university. When I arrived, there were over 90 students which left only a few empty chairs in the lecture hall. I enjoyed teaching. I had developed a good relationship with the University and was the "go to" guy for creating special programs when grant money became available within the social work department. I flourished as an academic, achieving two master's degrees and a Ph.D. I felt compelled to give back what I had learned and what I had experienced as a practicing professional.

My lectures did not malinger in pretentiousness. It was about cultivating an interactive learning environment. I was bent on motivating students to rip open the door to critical thinking and hopefully dispel some of their socially indoctrinated ideas about racism, sexism and ableism. The chairperson of the department was the epitome of what a social worker was expected to be. She was intuitive, knowledgeable, empathic, caring and savvy. She also gave me a license to teach as I saw fit.

As I stood at the podium organizing my notes, a

nagging feeling that something was wrong began to develop. I started scanning the classroom until a student posed a question about the origins of cremation. I responded with—

"An interesting piece of information about cremations is that evidence shows the practice of burning the body of the dead to ashes began during the early Stone Age in Europe and the Near East. It spread to the Roman Empire until Christianity replaced it with earth burials unless, of course, the person died from a plague."

As I lectured, I met the eyes of one of the students, and each time our eyes made contact, I felt increasingly anxious. I continued lecturing.

"Cremation as we know it began a little over six hundred years ago with the development of a dependable chamber. Almost half of all deaths end up in cremation, and that number is expected to keep rising."

The lecture went on for almost two hours. I never stopped looking in the general direction of that male student. In my eagerness to identify the student, I ended class abruptly. Students were milling out, and I started walking towards the male student, who, upon seeing me, moved faster toward the door.

I called out, "Hey, I need to talk to you!"

He stopped briefly and pulled open one side of his blazer, exposing a holstered gun. I came to a standstill. Wordless and with a smirk on his face, he quickly walked out of the room. I waited a minute, then walked to the main entrance just in time to see him jump into a waiting car that sped off and barely missed hitting a group of students crossing the street.

Shaken, I left the University, drove slowly and then fast, constantly looking in my rear-view mirror to see if I was being followed. University protocol demanded that I report the incident to campus police; however, I chose not to. Something told me to keep things to myself for now. I decided to drive up to my house in the Poconos and once settled in bed, I stared at the loaded 9mm semiautomatic Ruger lying on my nightstand.

I was licensed to carry a concealed firearm in Pennsylvania as well as New Jersey and New York. Social work practice had drastically changed. Almost all professional helpers who routinely practiced in the field were able to obtain gun carry permits after documenting

16 hours of gun range training. Decades ago, it was routine for social workers, doctors, physical therapists and nurses to go into all types of extremely dangerous neighborhoods unarmed to treat patients. Back then, carrying a handgun would have seemed ridiculous and contrary to our professional ethics and values. Things changed, though, largely due to the "growing economic divide," the affluent were no longer envied by the masses; they were hated.

Social desperation had set in and changed the rules of social engagement. People of means no longer wore extravagant clothes or drove fancy cars unless they had private security. It was not unusual to be spit on or have your car tires slashed or worse if you felt the need to flaunt your riches. Added to decades of simmering conflict between the government and marginalized residents, New York City was ripe for a cataclysmic event. Things went chaotic 80 years ago when a white cop killed two young black youth who were doing nothing more than taking a shortcut through a dark alley to their medical school.

When the grand jury refused to indict the cop, the city and its outlying boroughs went mad with rage. For an entire week, rioting and looting ensued, with hundreds arrested. A few days later, that same cop disappeared. He returned a week later, claiming that he had been kidnapped right off the street. He wouldn't go into the details; however, after being interviewed by internal affairs, word got out that he had been held by an unidentified group who physically and psychologically tortured him.

The cop willingly resigned from the force vowing never to work again in law enforcement. In the months that followed, there were several out-of-state high profile incidents where minority youth became victims of "death by cop." In each and every case, the cops were not indicted. Every one of the cops disappeared only to turn up a week later, mentioning an unidentified group.

To add more mystery to the events, each cop immediately resigned swearing to never again work in law enforcement. During the next year, every month, a major social media site was hacked. Pictures of unarmed Black, White and Hispanic youth killed by law enforcement agencies were displayed, ending with the following message:

"The days of tolerating the racist and discriminatory practices of law enforcement are over. Our society has allowed the practice of death by cop to become as commonplace as public lynchings were in early America. Black and poor youth are not the depraved monsters our education system, government and media portray. The evil lies with those who would subjugate and divide you."

"There are groups within law enforcement intoxicated with power believing they are excluded from being accountable for their actions. There are influential people in public and private positions who abuse power and demonstrate indifference to the masses who depend upon them. Force will be met with force. Too many will die waiting for the moral conscience of the elite to change. From here on, anyone who abuses the power entrusted to them by the citizenry will be immediately corrected by The Brotherhood of Justice."

The effect of that monthly mantra caused most public entities to "think first" and awakened the practice of public assembly in many groups around the country. The cops were in checkmate. The number of incidents of 'modern-day lynching by cop' were reduced to zero. As a social worker, I was amazed. It was the first time in history that a social ill was thoroughly and perfectly eradicated. The cops were scared, and the media neither endorsed nor criticized the vigilante tactics.

The *Brotherhood* of *Justice* didn't stop there; they focused the same tactics on random government officials guilty of crimes against the public yet exonerated by the court system. This initiative significantly reduced political indiscretions, but the cessation of the habit of politicians taking bribes was both formidable and unyielding. *The Brotherhood of Justice* continued their crusade despite being on the FBI's most dangerous list. In the end, crimes committed by politicians decreased dramatically.

All at once, there was a rustling sound outside my window. I quickly turned off the lights and slowly, very carefully pulled the curtain to the side while releasing the safety on my handgun. I saw a set of eyes shining between the trees and realized they belonged to a deer walking across my yard. I took a deep breath to help slow down my heart rate and put the safety back on. Looking at the cold, dark gun in my hand reminded me of the incident that drove me to own a gun.

Five years ago, a male and female EMS crew responded to the murder-suicide of a well-liked married elderly couple living in the East New York part of Brooklyn. The couple left a note indicating that poverty and hunger had won out and dying was their best option.

They ended their note with "We suffer no more."

The male EMS worker from the responding crew made a remark he would never live to regret. He said in a fairly loud voice, "What a fucking waste of our time." That remark was heard by several family members of the dead couple.

This isolated incident became the fuel to ignite the angst held by hundreds of thousands of people living on the economic and emotional edge. After the crowd beat the male EMS worker to death, violence spread like hellfire. Tens of thousands were rioting until hundreds of thousands took to the streets, causing wanton destruction. There was looting and raping in every borough and county in New York. There was little the local, state or federal agencies could do besides stand, watch and try to contain the wild bloodletting orgy. They were vastly outnumbered.

Eventually, when things died down, the playing field

for professionals working in the field underwent a 180-degree turn. Obtaining a gun carry permit became a legal option for any licensed professional working in New York State. Professional meant only those who were licensed by the state and had attained at least a graduate degree. So, mailmen, delivery persons and the like were on their own. They tried every legal avenue to obtain the right, but the powers that be were firm in their decision to exclude them. I placed my handgun on the nightstand.

I switched off the night table lamp and turned to a nightly New York news channel. The words *Breaking News* flashed on the screen. I turned up the volume in time to hear a reporter in lower Manhattan talking about a crime scene. A black SUV could be seen in the background. I turned up the volume.

"The body of Richard Brown, the Assistant Chief Pathologist for New York City, was found in his car, the apparent victim of an attempted carjacking." Mr. Brown's body was found only hours ago, slumped over the wheel of his late model Range Rover with two bullet holes to his head. There were no witnesses."

I raced toward the TV in disbelief and stood inches

from the screen. I was paralyzed, staring at the pictures of Rick's car and the blood on the car seat. I was trying to listen to the reporter, his mouth was moving, but I couldn't hear his words above the screaming. I put both hands on my head and cocked my head to the side. Then it hit me, I was the one screaming, screaming at the top of my lungs.

I stood mortified as if all the suffering in the world had just been uploaded into my heart and soul. My head was splitting in two; I wanted revenge, wanted to kill whoever did it. It dawned on me, while they were watching me in class, they were murdering Rick. All kinds of scenarios ran amuck inside my mind.

Part of me wanted to contact the police to see if anything I knew would help find Rick's killers. But for some reason, Rick didn't trust his own police department. For all I knew, someone from law enforcement was responsible for killing him. I wasn't buying the idea of a random carjacking, not for a second.

I fought the natural impulse to call Rick's wife Wendy. I couldn't bring myself to offer condolences, knowing full well the role I played in all of this. Besides, right now, she and her children are going through their own personal hell. I needed the killers to suffer, knowing it wouldn't change much or bring Rick back. My guilt required a pound of flesh, an eye for an eye.

My knee-jerk response was to clean my gun, pack a larger caliber .357 magnum handgun in my shoulder bag along with a shortened 30/30 rifle. I added several boxes of ammo and fell into a fitful sleep. Mercifully, my dreams didn't focus on the grisly aspects of Rick's death or the real possibility that I was next. Instead, I dreamt of Antoinette during the early days and playing the guitar at Emma's apartment.

The beautiful smiles of Tanisha and Linda Lonegan were in my mind's eye when I woke the next morning, reminding me that one of the constant benefits of hospice work was attaining a realistic perspective on life. There was nothing, absolutely nothing, I could face in life that amounted to more than what hospice patients faced on a daily basis. I knew that my teaching and hospice careers would have to be put on hold until I found some answers. I had a moral obligation to protect my students and patients.

E.O.L (End of Life)

Chapter III: I Can See Clearly Now

Monday morning at 10:00 am, I arrived at the hospice office to attend the bi-weekly team meeting. This would be my last time in the company of the hospice team. I had been at my bank and closed all of my accounts. I had enough money to keep me going for a couple of years if it became a necessity. Having no one to talk to or confide in about my sudden turn of events was unnerving. Even in the company of my team members, I felt estranged. It was a familiar feeling I had seen countless times when patients let go of their family and friends and prepared for death.

All of the members of the hospice team were present in the small conference room. I watched them and listened to conversations spiked with laughing, snippets of information, thoughtful silence, and a general display of camaraderie born from working together through hundreds of deaths. I wanted to leave; I didn't belong there anymore. Holding back the panic that welled up inside me left me emotionally drained.

At 8:30 am sharp, the chaplain, nurses, social workers, doctors and the clinical director strolled to their respective seats, holding fervently to their steaming cups of coffee. As I thumbed mindlessly through my notebook, I exchanged glances with several of the nurses, chaplains, social workers and doctors, nodding my head and making an effort to smile. Sara was sitting at the opposite end of the conference table; her stare was ripping a hole in the side of my head. I gave her a quick, perfunctory nod as Sister Gladys blessed the meeting with a prayer. Called "Death," written by Kahill Gibran.

"Trust in the dreams, for in them is hidden the gate of eternity. For what is it to die but to stand naked in the wind and to melt into the sun? And what is it to cease breathing, but to free the breath from its restless tides that it may rise and expand and seek your holy one unencumbered? Only when you drink from the river of silence shall you indeed sing. And when you have reached the mountain top, then you shall begin to climb. And when the earth shall claim your limbs, then shall you truly dance."

The first order of business involved one of my long-standing patients, Mr. Dennis Gordon. The clinical coordinator was the first to speak.

"We need to talk about what we're going to do about this patient; the police found him passed out in his wheelchair on the sidewalk at 3:00 am and took him to the hospital. He stayed there until 8:00 am; they hydrated him, discharged and transported him home."

Without much subtlety, most of the eyes in the room shifted towards me as if I were the one who wheeled Dennis to the local bar and poured the alcohol down his throat. In response, I said in no uncertain terms—

"The man is a legless dying alcoholic; if he chooses to ask his neighbor to hoist him into his motorized chair so he can make his way to the pub, you know my views. So, let's not go there, not today. What I'm saying is not news to anyone here. It's the beginning of the month, and Gordon's got his monthly checks, and he does what alcoholics do when they have money: He drinks!"

"It would be better for everyone if he made it home to sleep it off or, better yet, go to an AA meeting. People think social workers are some kind of super-beings that can make people do the right thing. He'd been playing this scene long before hospice came aboard. If you feel uncomfortable, I'm here to tell you to multiply how you feel by 10; that's Dennis's daily reality. If anyone here has a suggestion, now is the time to speak; if not, I suggest we move on to something we can change." And we did.

After the 90-minute meeting, everyone was buzzing about the murder of Rick Brown. Though I agonized throughout the conversations, I said nothing, pretending to be interested. I was glad when the talk shifted to the *Methuselah* epidemic. One of the doctors thought it would eventually infect every human on the planet, and age 40 would become the new 80, which made everyone laugh. Sister Gladys made reference to the *Book of Revelations* and the *Seven Plagues.*

I left the meeting early and decided to pay a quick visit to Dennis Gordon to see how he was coping. He lived in a 14th floor apartment on West 145th St. in Manhattan.

The doorman immediately buzzed me in. I didn't bother to knock; Dennis's door was wide open. He was in bed smoking a cigarette, watching a television show about men who pay men to sleep with their wives. Dennis was a tall, bald and burly man. He had a grey beard, and a long, large nose sat on his small face as if it had been attached as an afterthought. He had small, keen blue eyes, the kind that looked right through you. He turned in my direction and smiled.

"You ever watch this shit? I can't get enough of it so, what does that say about me?" He laughed loud and hard, causing him to cough and wheeze for several seconds. I asked if he was all right, and he nodded, "Yes." Several weeks ago, I had a hell of a time explaining to him that his oxygen tank would have to be removed unless he stopped smoking. It was not an easy thing to do for someone diagnosed with lung cancer. The alternative was taking the risk that he would set himself on fire as well as his neighbors. I could still hear him cursing and spouting his favorite phrase the day the techs removed the oxygen from his apartment.

"We all have two choices: either you get busy living,

or you get busy dying!" He was quoting a long-forgotten actor named Morgan Freedman's line from the ancient movie "Shawshank Redemption." A visit with Dennis involved listening to his "war" stories. He was a former New York City homicide detective, never married and childless.

"Did I ever tell you how I lost my legs?" "No, not in detail."

He smiled and took a large gulp from his bottle of gin. I made myself comfortable.

"I was known as a tough, no-nonsense cop who played by his own rules. Ten years ago, a 9-year-old girl and three of her friends were playing jump rope at a park on the west side of Manhattan."

"Two late model Lincolns, the gas kind they had before this solar crap, pulled up to the sidewalk adjacent to the park, and several men got out of the cars and engaged in a transaction of the illegal kind. Things became heated and led to gunplay, killing a 9-year-old girl. That little girl was my niece, and two days after the funeral, the shooters were found dead, missing choice body parts. Of course, I got the blame.

I wanted to ask him the burning question; however, it was better not to know.

"The dead guy was an international crime boss. I didn't know those cocksuckers put a contract out on me. My partner and I had pulled up to a local waffle house when shots rang out. He took a bullet in the neck and went down. I was hit in the arm. I called for an ambulance and backup, then went after the shooter. I was closing in on him when I fell to the ground from loss of blood, and fell right under a tractor-trailer. Woke up the next morning and noticed my legs were gone. My partner survived, and we retired as heroes. There was a story on page 9 of the Daily News."

"Wow, "that's quite a story." "I've got another one for you."

I sat back on the chair and listened to Dennis talk about some very drunk rich guy buying drinks all night for everyone in the bar a few days ago.

"Yeah, and this guy, he never said his name told me he was worth hundreds of millions of dollars. He was 90 years old if he was a day; the wild part about it was that he made all that money in the last two years and had

Methuselah to thank for it!"

I raised my eyebrows and leaned forward.

"He was vague about how he made the money. I thought he was just blowing smoke up our asses. He said that the money came with a terrible price, like making a deal with the devil. Oh yeah, one more thing he said, the guy who sold him this pie in the sky opportunity went by the name, the Doctor, that's it, that's all I got."

"That's a hell of a lot, Dennis; thanks, you take care. I'll see you soon." "Alright, be careful, Jay."

Two hours later I was on my way to see the drunken rich guy in Dennis' story. I got his name from the bartender and googled his address and phone number. He answered the phone when I called and agreed to be interviewed about his successful career as a banker.

I sat in a posh living room, listening to Carmine Dispasio talk about his retirement from Citibank. He and his wife had lived a comfortable life. She died four years ago. She was hit by a fire truck on its way uptown to what was later discovered to be a false alarm. After burying the love of his life, he came out of retirement and, in less than three years, amassed his fortune along with a diagnosis of

Methuselah.

I stayed focused as I made casual conversation with Carmine. He was the first person diagnosed with *Methuselah* who was alert, oriented and verbal. Each time I tried to probe deeper into *Methuselah*; Carmine deftly avoided giving straight answers. It was a cat-and-mouse game to him. This was a golden opportunity to get answers; I decided to go for broke.

"Look, Carmine, I know about the drug you bought and how it helped you to make your fortune in a short time." Carmine turned on the best poker face he could muster up and sat for a few long seconds, motionless and speechless. I continued undaunted, "You may not be in the final stage of *Methuselah*, but let's face the facts." I stood up and walked towards him and raised my voice.

"You're a 60-year-old man; you easily look 30 years older. There are thousands of men and some women already dead from this disease. I need you to tell me about it. My friend is dead; he was killed because of this, *Methuselah*!"

Carmine let out a long and hearty laugh that echoed throughout the penthouse. I stood in disbelief, trying my best not to unleash my rage on him.

"So, you think you can take this on all by yourself? Well, I'm here to tell you in no small way, sonny, that there's nothing, absolutely nothing you can do to stem this tidal wave."

"This juggernaut goes to the top of every major institution in this country; every judicial and law enforcement agency has someone in it. You think it's isolated to just the United States. Make no mistake, my young professor. This is global! Many have died and will die. As a matter of fact, I'll probably be dead in 24 hours. I was told, no, I was promised death for what I've said so far."

Carmine stopped talking and listened as if he could hear someone else. Suddenly, he said, "Anyway, this world won't be here much longer; I'll tell you everything I know because I believe my wife is in heaven waiting for me, and the only way I'm going to get there is by cleansing my tainted soul. Young man, you need to know before I go on, that once you have your answers, it'll just be a matter of time before they kill you, too. Do we go on?" I nodded yes.

He talked for hours, explaining in vivid detail exactly what, how, when and why he had chosen to become a part of what he called the *Clear Conspiracy.* I listened intently and didn't interrupt him once. The more I heard, the more afraid I became. I wouldn't show it, but I'm sure he felt my fear. My mind caught every word, every nuance and change in tonality. In all, four hours passed, and when the conversation was over, we both knew we'd never meet again.

The *Clear Conspiracy* was monstrously huge and had worked its way deep into the bastions of power. Minutes later, I stood in Carmine's doorway, shaking his hand.

"Carmine, I'm going to take your advice, leave the city, and find someone who can help me. I know someone. I don't know how to thank you…"

Carmine raised both open palms, smiled and said, "You're thanking me for your own death sentence?"

"Carmine, I need to know something." Was it really worth it, I mean, losing all those years for money?"

He took a deep breath and replied, "When I lost my wife, money became my lover. It pleasured me like a lustful young girl, but in the end, its lack of substance left me lonely and unfulfilled. So, my answer is yes and no."

I took Carmine's advice and drove to the outskirts of the city, parked and brainstormed. I had friends at all levels of law enforcement. Carmine's story convinced me that no one in government could be trusted. Alone, I was a dead man. One idea kept pushing through, and try as I might to oppose it, I made the decision to let it through. I called my cousin Percy and arranged to meet later that afternoon in Brooklyn.

I looked up from my cup of tea at my cousin Percy, who was staring down at his cup of black coffee. He took a couple of sips. I knew he was wondering why I wanted to meet after all these years. I looked over at the other customers in the café so as not to look directly at him. The years had not been kind to him. He didn't look old for his age; he looked haggard, sullen, angrier.

Percy was my oldest cousin. He had 5 younger siblings all raised by a single mom. The daily reality of being raised in East New York Brooklyn, dependent on the welfare system, an absentee dad, and conscripted to use a food voucher card at the local bodega where his peers ridiculed him, made him feel socially inept. He started smoking cigarettes and drinking alcohol at age twelve, to quiet his nerves. He was drafted into the Marines at age 19 and did several tours; he liked to kill and discovered that he was very good at it. The higher his body count, the more accolades, medals and respect he received.

He was a former special ops soldier and the black sheep of our family, a family that rarely acknowledged each other. Percy might as well have been invisible. In the rare instances that anyone had to interact with him, they kept their conversations short. Behind his back, they called him a trained killer with PTSD and a potential human time bomb. No one wanted to get caught up in the collateral damage. My mother and I had reached out to Percy when he returned to civilian life. We were also treated as outcasts; in a sense, it was a natural coming together of family misfits.

I wasn't sure how to explain the details of the "*Clear Conspiracy.*" I was still trying to make sense of it myself. How do you tell someone that a drug that costs over a million dollars for one use was being sold to people so that they could become filthy rich and that the side effect was that their age would be accelerated? Who would believe that people would be willing to make that trade-off? I had to try to get through to Percy; I desperately needed his help.

"So, Cuz, what kind of trouble are you in this time?"

The trouble he alluded to happened over 15 years ago. At that time, I received a frantic call from my sister informing me that my mother's boyfriend, an ex-convict named Ronald, had severely beaten her. After rushing her to the ER, where she was stabilized, I immediately called Percy. After explaining the circumstances, an hour later, we met and drove to the Flatbush area of Brooklyn where Ronald was known to hang out.

Percy said, "I hope you got the balls for this; this ain't no game. If things go south, we might have to take this dude out. You ready for that, Cuz?" I stared him in the eye, trying to buy some time. The thought of killing Ronald, or anyone for that matter, terrorized me. I nodded my head and went back to staring at the approaching road.

We stopped at several bars, eyeballing the crowds and in the last bar on the strip, the bartender told us Ronald had been there only moments ago with one of the local prostitutes. I told the bartender that I was Ronald's nephew and had lost the keys to the apartment we shared. The bartender told us that he didn't care who I was. He said, "I don't like the guy, he's a scum bag, and if anything goes down with him, he deserves it."

He told me that he thought Ronald and the woman caught a cab to a diner further downtown. When we arrived at the diner, I saw them and pointed the couple out to Percy. Ronald was a big guy sitting in a booth with a skinny, dark-skinned black woman sporting a very red wig.

We waited in the car, 50 feet from the main entrance to the restaurant. The street lamp's light shined on Percy's face, outlining several deep scars that spread from the side of his forehead to just below his ear. We had talked for over an hour about every detail of the plan. Percy, as was his habit, chain-smoked cigarettes, never taking his eyes off the front door of the restaurant for more than a couple of seconds. To me, he seemed to be the epitome of calmness and patience. He was a hunter, waiting to trap his prey.

For me, the minutes were long and filled with anxiety. I struggled to be patient. Every now and then, Percy shot a quick look at me and a nod, which made the corners of my mouth rise and my heart beat faster. We waited for almost two hours, then finally the couple hit the street. Percy and I eased out of the car, just as we planned. I stayed near the car, and Percy approached the couple and saw that Ronald was wearing a large gold watch.

Percy said to Ronald, "Scuse me, bro, you got the time? Ronald looked at Percy, looked around and then looked down at his watch. Percy sucker punched him so hard in the side of his head that Ronald, all 250 pounds of him, fell like a bag of bricks.

I continued to look around to make sure that no one saw us and ran over quickly to help Percy drag Ronald's limp body into the back seat of my car. We threw him onto the rear seat; the seat was still sticky from my mother's blood. Ronald's date took flight frantically walking down the street without uttering a single sound or looking back. It all seemed surreal and frightening.

When Ronald woke up, he was tied to a metal chair, and we had a canvas bag wrapped around his entire head. He had the worst headache of his life, and the ropes burned his wrists, ankles and neck. He could hear whispered voices in the room and began to shout, “Hey, you over there, I need help. I’ve been kidnapped; I don’t know what’s going on.” “Some sick fucks left me in this place; please help me, please help me, PLEASE!”

Before he could utter the word “please” again, Percy sprung across the room and backhanded him so hard that Ronald’s head rocked back and forth several times before his chin came to rest on his breastbone, thinly toned whimpers escaped from his mouth. I saw frothy red saliva streaming down the sides of his mouth and neck.

We left him in that position for another hour. A few times, I wanted to tell Percy that I had changed my mind and that we could get in trouble. I fought the impulse because I knew I would not be able to stomach looking at my mother and sister, knowing that I chose to be noble and had turned the other cheek. Even more, I wouldn’t be able to face myself.

The savagery of the beating inflicted upon my mother was eerily reflected in the knuckles of Ronald’s two hands. They were swollen, bruised, framed in a purplish hue of torn flesh. It was our plan to stay anonymous and inflict as much pain and damage as possible onto Ronald without killing him. Ronald would never know his kidnappers or who had crippled both of his hands and injured his genitals with well-placed kicks.

I was not proud of what Percy did to Ronald; I felt totally responsible even though I had not participated in rendering the physical punishment. The truth was Percy and I were black men who knew we had to express our "Bigger" moments; Percy released his through his hands and I released my angst through my mind. All told, it did feel good to see Percy hitting Ronald.

I stirred my tea and looked up at Percy. He was looking around at the different faces in the coffee shop.

"So, Cuz, what's up, somebody trying to kill you? "Funny you should say that. Yeah, my life's in danger."

Percy sat up straight, leaned toward me, looked at me dead on and told me to start from the beginning and not to leave out one single detail. I started with the *Methuselah* epidemic, went on to Rick's involvement and death, the gunman in my class and my meeting with Carmine. An hour later, I sat back, mentally exhausted, looking at his face for a reaction.

"So, you don't know if all this is true? This is some

Sci-Fi, futuristic conspiracy shit you're talking about. Somebody's getting rich helping people to get richer and die early. And they do this by injecting a drug which programs them?"

"Yeah, that about sums it up. The drug is called *Clear*, It helps people to see what they need to do. The closest experience would be tripping on acid.

A brain on acid allows unprocessed information into the conscious mind. *Clear* goes one better and travels to all parts of the brain. This creates experiences "of already visited and already experience or déjà vu. Deja vu is when someone finds themselves in a situation that they had mentally lived through before; everything is familiar to them. *Clear* helps the user to see the next step; it produces future sight, a type of extrasensory perception."

"What? Okay slow down, back up, you're losing me."

The couple at the next table gave us a quick look and then returned to their conversation. I waited a moment to make sure that no one was listening.

"Okay, try this on for size. Somehow, the people who are selling this drug are able to psychologically implant a personal goal the user has chosen. What's really scary is that Carmine, was dying from *Clear* and didn't really know how it works. *Clear* users want wealth and power, even though they were told it could be used to attain anything that's humanely possible."

"Okay, okay, so why should we care if a few rich white dudes shorten their lives? Our people have been dying from drugs for hundreds of years. Who's doing anything about them? Who gives a shit about these rich jokers? Let the fools die like the rest of the suckers working themselves to death."

"Percy, it's more than that; this *Clear Conspiracy* is responsible for the kidnappings of hundreds, maybe thousands of people, including children. I'm not sure how, but they're connected. It's not about race, color or status. You've been talking for years about government conspiracies, covert operations, and planned assassinations. Why is it so hard to imagine this?"

I watched him attempt to speak, then he stopped, cocked his head to the side. The look on his face transformed from curiosity, disbelief, astonishment and slowly, ever so slowly, to serious consideration.

While Percy was having his epiphany, I checked my

phone. It had been vibrating for the last 20 minutes; I saw three missed calls from Sara. I dialed her number, and when she answered, I could feel the stress in her voice.

"Hey Sara, are you okay?"

"Not really, I know you're on leave, but I don't know who else to call."

Painfully, she talked about her new hospice patient, a 6-month-old infant with hydrocephalus, also known as "water on the brain." If that wasn't enough, the child lived with her 15-year-old single undocumented mother in a high-crime public housing unit in the Bronx. There was a strong possibility that the baby's father was part of a notorious street gang called "The Tomahawks." The baby's mom was being vague about the father's involvement and whereabouts. Sara sensed trouble, and wanted to help the child, but knew she was putting herself in a dangerous situation.

Against my better judgment, I agreed to help. I told Percy and listened to his response, "Do what you gotta do, bro. Give me a call on this phone; it's got a built-in cell site. The cell signature changes every three minutes. It can't be traced or hacked."

"Really? I'm impressed."

"Let me know when you're ready to move on this *Clear* thing."

I nodded twice, ran outside, almost got into my car, then remembered that both Carmine and Percy said that would be suicidal considering what was going on. I caught a train to the Bronx.

When I arrived at the building, I saw Sara in her car talking on her phone. When our eyes met, she quickly hung up, gathered her nursing gear, stepped out of the car and locked the door. We hugged and proceeded into the vestibule of the building. We took off our SCBAs and grimaced from the stench of old urine.

When you saw me on the phone, I was talking to the head of security again and he said they want no part of The Tomahawks. (Tomahawks were brutal and have been known to savagely murder entire families for a $100.00 unpaid debt). The graffiti filled walls were a graphic reminder that we were in an unfriendly place. We tried unsuccessfully to hold our breaths while we waited for the snail-like elevator to creak to a stop in the lobby.

The door opened slowly, revealing days-old garbage

on the floor and something that looked and smelled like feces spread near the bottom of the metal walls. We headed towards the stairs. The door to the staircase was missing, along with most of the ceiling bulbs. The setting reminded me of an incident that happened last year. An armed female social worker was murdered while visiting a client in a public housing complex in Queens. The murder weapon was a chainsaw.

With that thought on my mind, I led the way up the dimly lit, foul-smelling staircase. We were careful not to touch the walls or the metal banister. The 4th floor was our destination, and things were going well until we rounded the corner of the third floor. Several bodies were strewn on the stairs. We looked at each other silently, hoping they were sleeping.

I took Sara's hand as we walked around the body of a young woman dressed in jeans and a very dirty jacket who smelled of alcohol and a god-awful sweet perfume. We looked for and saw the rise and fall of her chest, confirming she was alive. Loud snoring came from the next body. He was a man in his thirties with a heavy salt and pepper beard, dirty red slacks and reeked of old beer, cocaine and urine.

I stepped over him; however, Sara was not so sure-footed, and the heel of her boot brushed the guy's shoulder, startling him and causing him to reach out and latch his hand around Sara's ankle. She let out a muffled cry, and she tried to get him to release his grip; he held on tight. I quickly came down two steps and kicked his arm, freeing Sara. He cried out in pain, and when his now-opened eyes met mine, he decided it was in his best interest to go back to sleep.

The woman who opened the door to apartment 4N looked no older than 13 years of age; she looked very anxious. She ushered us in quickly and fastened several deadbolt locks. We followed her through the sparsely furnished apartment to a back room where the baby stared up from a small mattress on the floor.

When a baby or a child is placed on hospice, it never fails to suck out a part of your life's essence. The 6-month-old baby girl's head was too large for her frame, and her face was expressionless. She did not have the young cherubic features expected from an infant. Her countenance reflected a lifetime of pain and misery.

While Sara examined the baby, I spoke to Estela, the baby's mother, and after 20 minutes of listening to her speak in Spanish and broken English, I discerned that all of us in that apartment were in grave danger. From what I could understand, three weeks ago, she ran away from the apartment she shared with her baby's 34-year-old father. He was a long-time member of a local gang that dealt in drugs, guns and prostitution. They tried to get her hooked on the *New Red Heroin,* which had a high that lasted 72 hours, but she refused to take the bait. They still pimped her out and beat her on a regular basis.

After the baby was born, he ordered her to start prostituting again. She defied him by leaving with the baby along with thousands of dollars of the gang's money. She paid a slumlord two months' rent for this hole in the wall. Two days ago, when her baby stopped making sounds and movements, she went to the local ER and was told by the doctors her baby had six months or less to live. I quickly explained the situation to Sara and insisted that we leave as soon as possible. Without warning, there was an abrupt succession of hard knocking on the front door immediately followed by the frantic turning of the doorknob.

Estela sucked in a massive amount of air and then whispered, "Silencio, silencio por favor!"

That all-too-familiar feeling of numbing cold ran up and down my spine.

All at once, loud voices in the hallway were followed by an avalanche of kicks to the door. At most, we had 2-3 minutes before the deadbolts failed. Sara and Estela stared at the door, then at me, their faces frozen in terror.

My life flashed before my eyes; for a split second, I saw all of us dead on the floor of this empty apartment. I grabbed their shoulders and said.

"Get the baby; we're going down the fire escape!"

Thirty seconds later, Sara came out of the room, followed by Estela, tightly holding the blanketed baby in her arms. I had opened the kitchen window, and with Sara in the lead, I brought up the rear as we moved down the rickety metal stairs. The irony was that I had two handguns, which were virtually useless because getting safely to street level was all I could focus on. Finally, Sara, Estela and the baby reached the sidewalk, and I was stepping off the last rung of the ladder when it happened. There were heavy thumps on the fire escape above us; looking up, I saw three guys with guns in hand desperately scrambling down the metal stairs. We weren't going to make it to Sara's car.

"Sara, run around the corner before they start shooting! Get in your car, GET OUT OF HERE!

She wasn't budging; she gave me a questioning look.

"Save the baby, Sara, go on; there's no time! Please, I'll be all right."

I half turned to go back, and before my guns cleared their holsters; the sound of an Uzi machine gun shattered the air. I looked up, and the three guys were desperately clawing their way back up the fire escape. I looked back down and saw Percy spraying bullets and spitting words at the fleeing Tomahawks.

"What's up gang banger punks? I thought you wanted to play! Come on, there's three of you…oh, I get it; you only shoot women and sick babies."

The next couple of minutes were unreal. I stood in place and watched two of the gang bangers fall to the sidewalk; the sound of their bodies hitting concrete made me want to puke. They were still alive, but too broken up to move. Percy stepped over quickly and put three bullets into each of their heads. Then, he methodically shot out every security camera within range. Apparently, while this was going on, Sara had the presence of mind to get to her car. She pulled up, and Percy and I piled in. Once in the car, Percy told Sara not to panic and drive normally.

Sara dropped us off downtown; I suggested she take the baby to the hospital and get the police involved. She told me by tomorrow, Estela and the baby would be in a safe house for domestic violence survivors. She hugged me so hard I had to pry her arms off. She shot a glance at Percy and said, "Thank you." I watched her car pull off; Estela was in the back seat waving goodbye at us. We set out for the train and disappeared down the steps. Thankfully, the next train arrived in less than five minutes.

Percy sat with his legs crossed and outstretched with a satisfied look on his face. He seemed oblivious to the other passengers on the train. For me, the shock of the near-fatal incident in the apartment was beginning to wear off. Percy turned, looked at me, turned away and closed his eyes.

"Percy, all I can say is thank you," "That was a freebie, Cuz; we're family."

The train was crossing the bridge to Brooklyn. I didn't know where we were headed, had no plans for tomorrow and felt severed from the life I knew. All things considered, I was glad everyone that mattered, came out alive.

Chapter IV: What Doesn't Kill You Makes You a Survivor

The next morning, I woke up rubbing my stiff neck; it took a few seconds to remember where I was. The flocked wallpaper, cheap pictures, and numerous cigarette burns on the nightstand made it real. Yesterday, I had gotten off the train a few stops before Percy and checked into this dive of a motel. Percy said it was a good place to chill since only people cheating on their significant others or hookers and their customers frequented it. I was glad they took cash and asked no questions.

My stomach was empty and making strange sounds. After showering and dressing quickly, I stepped out of the den of iniquity and welcomed the warm sun on my face. I pulled my hoodie down to cover the part of my face left bare by my SCBA and made my way to the back of a coffee shop two blocks away. I ordered a small feast and then called Percy on the phone he had given me.

"Hey Percy, how's it going?"

"Everything's good so far. So, Professor, what's your game plan for today?"

"I need to access my e-mail. I'm going to find a library." "Sounds good, bro; think smart, call me later."

"Will do."

I was in and out of the library in 20 minutes, then rode the "F" train to Coney Island, trying to make sense of my "out of control life." I came to the conclusion that my chances of surviving this nightmarish tribulation would be much improved if I were to become more proactive than reactive. I had received several messages from students, and numerous messages from Sara marked urgent. All of her messages had the same theme. She wanted to know what kind of danger I was involved in. The message that attracted my curiosity was from Phillip Lonegan. He wanted me to call him immediately. He went as far as to say it was a matter of life and death. He left his personal cell number and, in no uncertain terms, told me to block my number.

I took a quick look at the local news thread, and just as I suspected, there was a report about someone breaking into the penthouse apartment of retired banker Carmine Despasio and throwing him off his balcony. They didn't even try and make it look like an accident. He fell to his death. I knew I was next in line, so calling Phillip, was a priority. I dialed his number.

He answered on the first ring. "Phillip Lonegan"

"Hi Phillip, it's Jay."

"Jay! Man, am I glad to hear from you." "Uh, you mentioned life or death?"

"And I'm not just talking about yours and mine." "What's going on, Phil?"

"One-word Jay, *Clear,* we have to meet today."

The prospect of meeting with Phillip gave me both hope and fear. Maybe he could shed more light on things. At the same time, I was highly skeptical and knew better than to show up alone. I needed Percy to watch my back, however, after yesterday's killings in the Bronx, getting him to travel from his safe haven in Brooklyn to meet someone I wasn't sure I could trust wasn't going to be easy.

"Okay, Phil, let's meet at the last place we saw each other in four hours."

"Done; see you there and be careful; things are not safe."

"You got that right."

I had to prepare, so I called Percy and filled him in on my plans to meet Phillip.

"How do you know we can trust this guy? This could be a setup and that means game over."

I could see that talking about this on the phone wasn't going to work so I suggested we talk face to face. We decided to meet at the train station at Eastern Parkway in Brooklyn. When I arrived at the station, Percy was there, and he wasn't alone. There were a couple of guys hanging back on the platform staring at us. One looked White and the other Hispanic. I shook hands with Percy.

"Who are those guys?"

"Let's just say, they're going to ride shotgun while we

hash this out. Now tell me more about this Phillip dude?"

In detail, I explained how I met Phillip, the phone calls I eavesdropped on, and his mother's concern that Phillip was more than he appeared to be, as well as her fear that he was in over his head in something dangerous. I ended with Phillip's ties to the government and my suspicions that he knew all about *Clear* and, more than likely, the people who were kidnapped.

"He knows more about my involvement than I do. I have to meet him." "How do you know that the government or the guys behind this *Clear Conspiracy* didn't find out about your relationship with him, and they're on their way to snuff everybody out?"

"To be honest, I don't know. My guts and instincts tell me that Phillip has the missing information. Anyway, I don't have a choice. What do I have to do to get your help?

He smiled slyly, saying, "I'm glad you asked, Cuz."

He waved over the white guy, and they jumped from the platform to the center of the tracks. Then he waved for me to join them, and I hesitated, wondering what they were up to. It seemed crazy to walk on the tracks.

"Come on down, Cuz, we need to get off of these tracks before a train comes. We got a little spot we're gonna walk to. I don't have to tell you to stay away from the third rail."

I jumped down and followed, keeping my distance from them. They walked fast, and I had to hustle to keep up. We went down the tunnel to a small substation area about 200 yards from the station. There was a flat open space about 20X20 feet surrounded by locked electrical panels. A couple of very large rats scurried away in the dimly lit area. I started to get a bad feeling.

"Cuz, to be honest with you. I like how you handled the situation in the Bronx the other day. I'm not sure you see the "big picture." My guys need proof that you got skills. They ain't got no faith in a college professor slash social worker. You're talking about taking on bad guys with ground troops and serious firepower. This C*lear* Conspiracy is no nonsense. We're going to war, and when the shit hits the fan, we need to know that you're adding, not taking away our chances to stay alive. I'm talking hand to hand bro. This ain't no movie where somebody's going to step in and save your ass!"

I took a moment to reflect on his words. It hit me as if I had put my hand into a raging fire. I was in a different world. Here, you had to prove your worth and hold your own. It was a paradigm shift, and I was a new piece of the puzzle.

He must've told his guys that I had a third-degree black belt in Tae Kwon Do. They wanted to play gladiator. The guy had already taken off his coat, SCBA, and was stretching his arms and legs under the single lightbulb that hung from a wire on the concrete ceiling, causing it to sway with the air currents of the tunnel. He was a couple of inches taller than me, about the same age, and had me by about 30 pounds, most of it muscle.

He didn't smile; he was all business. I took off my jacket, hat and SCBA immediately feeling angry that my life had taken this turn. I could hear the Korean voice of my Sensei. He was saying that anger and fear were the true enemies. I had to get focused. I took my time stretching my arms and legs, hoping my delaying tactics would piss this guy off.

It did, and he side-kicked me into the wall. I was able to block most of the kick with my forearm. He seemed to be surprised at my quickness. With fists tightly clenched, we circled each other. His face was scarred like Percy's, a reminder of his warrior past. When his fist hit my ribs, it took most of the breath out of my lungs, and my outstretched hand kept me from collapsing. A faint smile formed on his face.

I stayed true to my training and struck at vital areas when I could.

I was quicker than him and had more stamina; after blocking countless blows and constantly moving out of his striking distance, I began to slow down. I needed an opportunity, and when I saw him make a move to get rid of the sweat in his eyes by shaking his head and momentarily blinking rapidly three times. I anticipated the next succession of blinking.

I lowered my body, took several very quick steps, and front-kicked him in the groin, which brought his head down, and I smashed my knee deep into his nose. I didn't break it, but it spurted blood like a busted water balloon. I didn't stop there; I grabbed his bloody head bringing him to the ground in a chokehold.

In my peripheral vision, I could see Percy yelling at

me, I was oblivious until I realized that I was being pulled off of his neck. I wiped the sweat from my forehead with my bloody hands. I felt I was in a dream. I watched Percy at the other end of the space, helping to revive the man I had tried to kill. I laid down with my back on the hard-cold ground and tried to quiet the trembling that racked my body. I had let the brute out; it had been years since I had felt the beast in me.

A very large rat appeared and scurried over to where the blood had pooled. It began to lap it up, until Percy's boot came down to crush its head. Eventually, when I sat up, they were staring at me, I wondered if, like me, they were questioning my sanity. The wry smile on Percy's face answered that question.

The anger that had escaped from me had several beginnings. Number one was the racist dogma that existed in all major institutions in America. A close second was the fact that the number one killer of black youth was, in fact, after all these centuries, still black youth. As a teenager, I was constantly bombarded by the insecurity of life, social challenges, and the limitations imposed by growing up in a single-parent household engulfed in lies and domestic violence.

The word "nigger" seems to be immortal. It just will not die. It has survived for over 700 years. It is generally defined as, a contemptuous name for a black or dark-skinned person. It clearly was created by whites.

—Over 500 years ago, James Baldwin wrote, "no American Negro exists, who does not have his private Bigger Thomas living in his skull."

This is in reference to the novel **Native Son** (1940) by African-American author Richard Wright. The novel describes the story of 20-year-old Bigger Thomas, a Black American youth living in utter poverty. The novel's depiction of Bigger and his motivations to commit crimes draws a clear path to systemic inevitability. As Bigger's lawyer points out, there is no escape from this destiny for his client or any other Black American, since they are the necessary product of the society that formed them as James Baldwin so eloquently put it, *"what you say about someone, reveals who you are."* As a black man and as a social worker, I've always known that racist and ignorant white men were the "niggers." I grew up empathizing with the impoverished, the disabled, and the elderly; they seemed to have no one but themselves. My career choices helped me to maintain my focus on sanity keeping my "Bigger" moments in check.

I glanced at my watch, which thankfully was still functioning; I had less than two hours to prepare for the meeting with Phillip. We donned our SCBA's and I helped Percy assist the guy out of the space and back to the platform at the station. Halfway there, the Hispanic guy came running down the track; obviously, he seemed worried by the way things turned out, but he didn't say anything. He shot me a dirty look and led the way. Once on the platform, we quickly made our way to the street. We were attracting a lot of attention from the subway riders. Thank God there were no police around. I noticed all the cameras in the station had been sprayed with black paint.

We entered a van that had a lot more than the usual number of solar panels on the roof. When I entered, I saw why; the interior resembled a mini command center. They blindfolded me. We drove in silence for 30-40 minutes, parked, and passed through what smelled like a laundry mat and into a back room. I heard a door slide open and once we had passed through it, my blindfold was removed.

The room we had entered was quite large, brightly lit, and full of activity. There were three hallways leading to stairs to other parts of what appeared to be a very large private house. What struck me was that every man and woman was focused on an activity. There were no side conversations or people milling around. No one gave me more than a glance.

I was told to have a seat while they tended to Tony's (the guy) injuries. I focused on the movements of the men and women in the room. Some wore a very familiar uniform; I had seen those colors before. That same cold feeling began to run up and down my spine. Then I remembered, these were the colors displayed when *The Brotherhood of Justice* hacked the social media sites! I was in their headquarters. Everyone moved methodically and seemed to only speak when they needed to. Some sat at desks typing, and others studied huge video screens on the wall. All wore side arms.

When Percy returned, he told me I needed to get checked out by the medic. He led the way down one of the hallways and down a flight of stairs into a room that would put most hospital emergency rooms to shame. I was introduced to the female doctor, and received treatment for the cuts and bruises on my face and arms; the results of the x-rays revealed no fractures and no concussions. Percy returned with the Hispanic guy, who introduced himself as Manny.

While Percy stood by, Manny explained that *The Brotherhood* was made up of former military and law enforcement personnel. They were the answer to corruption, and that I would be surprised if I knew which levels of government and which corporations were sponsoring them. What I really wondered was why I was being given such classified information, but I thought it wise to keep my thoughts to myself.

Percy interrupted, "Hey, Cuz, looks like we're gonna back you on this meeting you have."

We talked, discussed strategies, and made contingency plans.

They dropped me off half a mile from my meeting point, which gave them time to arrive before me and get into position. I walked toward Manhattan's west side. I was approximately five blocks from where Phillip had tossed Linda's ashes into the river. I was scared even though I knew that Percy and Manny were on opposite sides of the street, no more than 200 feet away, and heavily armed. The radio receiver in my ear was extremely small and powerful and had been painted to match my skin color.

I had mixed feelings about getting involved with *the Brotherhood of Justice.* They were heroes in the communities and criminals in the eyes of the law; they'd been on the FBI's most wanted list for years. My life had become so messed up in such a short amount of time, and all because of this *Clear Conspiracy.* Circumstances demanded that I accept help from anyone that would offer it. The fact I was allied with *The Brotherhood* actually helped spark a belief, small as it was, that I could possibly live through this.

The sound and urgency in Percy's voice transported my mind back to the matters at hand.

"Radio check, bro, Jay, are you hearing me?"

"I hear you."

"When you see Phillip, stop and make him come to you. We need to position ourselves, okay?"

"Okay, I understand." I felt nothing; when I looked deeper inside myself, I realized that fear had numbed me.

The thoughts of actually dying in the next few minutes pervaded my mind. It wasn't death that I feared, that had been resolved years ago. I didn't want to die for no damn good reason. The .357 revolver in my waist holster added a degree of comfort; it was designed to inflict major damage at close range. I prayed that I would not be forced to use it. If Phillip was here for the wrong reason, he was going to die today. I still felt the need to avenge Rick's death, and nothing and no one was getting in my way. I whispered.

"I'm a block away, nothing yet." "I hear you, Cuz."

—When I was a kid, my friends and I once climbed a rocky stone pillar to get to the top of a 200-foot-high train trestle that spanned a river. When we reached the top, we looked down at the jagged river bed below. We dared each other to climb out on the metal trestle and hang over the edge using only our hands and arms. None of us wanted to be labeled a chicken, so we climbed out as if we were on the monkey bars in the park. We stopped when we were about 5 feet from the rocky edge; we held on for dear life, too afraid to look down at our dangling feet. One slip would have guaranteed death.

I felt the same now, only much less in control. I scanned the area in a slow-moving arc and saw Philip approaching in the distance. He was not alone; there was a man with him. I stopped walking and put my hand inside my jacket pocket, which thanks to Percy's advice, had the bottom cut out, allowing me to freely grip my handgun.

Barely moving my lips, I whispered, "he's not alone; he brought another guy!"

"We see them, when they're near that statue on the right; tell them to stop, make sure they hear you. If they keep coming, we're all going to get busy."

"Okay, okay."

—On the roof of an apartment building, 400 yards away from where Jay was meeting Philip, Percy was thinking that he had a problem. There were two, not one person approaching. He saw that Jay was standing his ground and he decided to do the same. His finger was pressed tightly to the trigger. If he had to, he could snuff both of them in less than a second. He dared not blink or breathe as they approached Jay.

"That's close enough, Phillip!"

Phillip and his associate stopped dead in their tracks and quickly looked at each other; then, their eyes began scanning the area high and low.

"Jay, what's with the cloak and dagger routine?"

"That question seems more appropriate for me to ask. Who's your friend Phillip?"

"Oh, don't be worried about him. This is my driver and business partner; his name is Marcos.

So… this was Marcos, the voice on the other end of Phil's cell. Marcos stood roughly 5 foot 6 inches and was a wiry 150 pounds. He was well into his fifties and dressed in a close-fitting black suit. The outline of a very large handgun was prominent just below his left shoulder. Their SCBA's looked military issued, designed to do more than filter air. He didn't utter a word, preferring to take his cues from Phil.

"What now?"

"Well, first, you can stop calling me Phillip and call me Phil." "Okay, done."

"And second, we got to get our asses off of the streets.

You have no idea how much you're involved in all of this. They're doing everything they can to find and eliminate you. There are more than enough cameras out here to identify you. Marcos is going to get the car, okay?"

Percy whispered in my ear.

"Hey, Cuz, no sweat. Tony's in the van a block away, he'll pick us up, and we'll follow. Tell Phil his driver is to stay local and drive at the speed limit through commercial streets. Make sure you sit in the front seat facing the driver and don't release your finger from the trigger, not even for a second. If you have to, take headshots."

"Okay, but before I get in the car, I have some conditions."

After repeating Percy's instructions to Phil, he agreed to the terms, so we waited for Marcos.

Within minutes, he returned, and I stood amazed as Marcos drove up in a "*Behemoth*." It was a military-grade vehicle designed to resemble a smaller version of a stretch limo. It had small, dense windows made from a compound of bulletproof glass and diamond crystals. The car's body was covered with a foot of a reinforced alloy of chromium and tungsten, making it able to withstand the impact and heat from smaller air to surface missiles.

Percy sounded impressed, "God damned, do you know what one of those costs?"

The *Behemoth's* sophisticated radar system could detect the approach of inflight missiles hundreds of miles away, giving its occupants time to get underground or stop and prepare for contact. Preparation for a missile concussion involved flipping several switches, which sent huge overlapping plates made of nanomaterials that completely covered the vehicle from top to bottom.

If that wasn't enough, four huge titanium-tipped drills were poised to open like huge telescoping drills and anchor the vehicle ten feet into the ground.

The Behemoth was the choice vehicle for Arab Kings, Prime Ministers, Presidents, and leaders of industry. It was powered by two large electromechanical engines, one under the hood and the other in the trunk. Each engine produced 750 horsepower, which propelled the 12-thousand-pound Behemoth 0-60mph in six seconds and topped out at 150 miles an hour. Phil was looking at my reaction.

"When you used to visit my mother, we talked about

cars; you know quite a bit about them."

"Yeah, I know a thing or two; let's get inside."

Once inside, we removed our SCBAs, and I marveled at the technology and craftsmanship of the vehicle's interior; it resembled the cockpit of a fighter jet, and I noticed that it had impressive offensive weaponry. Phil was quietly studying my every move and reaction. He looked tired and worn, not the energetic, tough-talking guy I had known him to be. I wondered what he knew and how he was involved in the conspiracy. He didn't wait long to start filling in the answers. He made direct eye contact with me and didn't look away for a second while he spoke.

"Let's get right to it. Twenty years ago, a former business associate at the Pentagon invited me to a private meeting, saying it had the potential to change lives. I'm the questioning type. I don't usually step into something without doing a little fact finding. All my associate knew was some New York-based consortium had discovered a "genie in a bottle" that guaranteed a filthy rich life. Now, he was no dummy, and to be honest, I was intrigued and decided to go."

"A week later, it was on a Saturday night at 8:00 pm in a warehouse on the lower west side of Manhattan."

"Twenty-third street and ninth avenue," Marcos added.

"Yeah, that was it; well, when we got there, I was surprised to see over 100 of the who's who of the New York State financial scene. There were CEOs of million-dollar companies, hedge fund owners, judges, high-level government administrators, and the like. It was a lavish affair boasting fine American and European cuisine served by beautiful female waiters in sexy attire. There were several men working security and taking their orders from this one guy. He was black, tall in stature, and polished, but, in a fake way. He was a slick talker, and reminded me of a sophisticated car salesman. When everyone was fed and liquored up, he went into his pitch."

"He said he was representing his partner, who was the inventor of a product that would make multi-millionaires of everyone in the room, and a million dollars could buy that opportunity. When pressed for details, he became tight-lipped. He said it was a complex procedure that involved a new chemical that could best be explained by his partner who he called "the doctor." He added that their clinical trials were over, and the results were amazingly successful. Almost everyone was interested in meeting "the doctor," everyone except me and a couple of others. We left before the show was over."

"Now, here's the shit! I read the newspaper every day, and since that day, everyone at that meeting became multi-millionaires; some became, billionaires. I have a habit of checking out the obituary columns it's a morbid hobby of mine. Let me tell ya, all of those poor fuckers have died. Most of them are from advanced old age.

Marcos interjected, "The *Methuselah* killed them."

Marcos wasn't missing a word as we, casually drove through 57th Street and 5th Avenue; his eyes were glued to the rear-view mirror. I released my grip on the trigger and stared out the window, watching storefronts go by and the occasional group of people wielding signs describing some facsimile of "the day of reckoning is upon us." I thought about the unrest and protests in the streets firm in my resolve that the escalation of angst, violence, and deaths was being caused by *Clear*.

Marcos began pulling the car over, and I kept my eyes

on his hands. Phil put one hand in his pocket, and I got ready to put a bullet in their heads.

Phil said quickly, "I wanted Marcos to pull over so we could explain our involvement with *Clear*. We'll tell you what we know, and then you tell us what you know, deal?"

I nodded my approval. Phillip told me pretty much everything Carmine told me the day before he was murdered. Neither of them knew who "the doctor" was or how *Clear* was created. The irony was that people worked hellish hours trying to get ahead of the pack. They worked at increasingly higher levels losing sleep, eating crap foods, forgoing exercise and family time. In the end, a shorter life and medical issues were usually the final outcome. *Clear* seemed to be a shortcut to riches and also guaranteed an early grave.

"Marcos was my right-hand man at the agency; we retired and set up a consulting firm. He's been digging around for the last few years. Lately, he's been listening to cyber chatter, and your name came up more than once."

"My name, so, why me?"

"I don't pull punches, and I'm not going to start now. Someone wants you dead in the worst way, my friend."

"Funny, if you told me this a few days ago, I would've said you had me mixed up with someone else. What makes me so special?"

"That's what we want to know, but before we go there, there's something else we heard."

Marcos added his voice, "Mr. Jay, I have friends in key places that hear things. These people behind this conspiracy have killed before. They want you dead. But there is more, much more."

"Like what?"

Marcos and Phil looked at each other, and Phil nodded to Marcos to keep talking.

"They're warehousing the missing people."

"What are you talking about, the kidnapped people, are they alive? There must be thousands of people, hundreds of kids missing. Where are they?"

Marcos said flatly, "That, we don't know yet."

Phil looked directly into my eyes and told me he suspected that I knew more than I realized. He let me know that through the years, the guy who recruited customers for *Clear* went underground with his drug dealing.

Phil added, "His name is Carl Stevens. Twenty years ago, Carl was a low-level drug dealer in Harlem. He started using his own shit and got sloppy. The Feds picked him up on a drug buy and charged him with possession with intent to distribute. The prosecutor was pushing for ten years, and Carl's hotshot lawyer got him 18 months of mandated drug rehab, go figure. Anyway, he was remanded to a therapeutic community in the Bronx called "New Horizons."

Phil and Marcos were studying my reaction. The name "New Horizons" surprised me; Phil and Marcos took note by quickly glancing at each other. I thought about the name Carl Stevens "saying it several times in my mind and then the emotions and memories came rushing in.

They were waiting for me to say something, and I didn't disappoint them. Twenty years ago, I was at New Horizons as a social work intern. During my 3rd month there, Carl Stevens arrived for treatment, and I was next in rotation to do the intake. I'll never forget that maniac. At age ten, his mother was murdered, and just two years later, someone murdered his father and his father's girlfriend. He went to live with an alcoholic uncle and, at the tender age of 13, quit school and became a drug dealer. He had learned how to make "zero-zero," a liquid hallucinogenic drink so called due to its intense psychedelic properties. The high was rumored to last for 8 hours, just enough time to recover and be ready for work the next day."

"I remember him like it was yesterday. He was a scary bastard, not so much for his size; It was the malevolent evil that emanated from him. That's what bothered me. When he chose to look at you, You could smell the poison that ran through his veins. I remember, as a young teen, he terrorized his neighborhood with a Ruger handgun; even the big kids steered clear of him. He pistol-whipped anyone who got in his way."

"Carl was in his thirties when he got to New Horizons in the Bronx. He looked burnt out when he arrived, and after a few weeks of rest and food, he gained weight like all the others. Unlike the others, he became more loathsome and vicious every day. He didn't follow the rules, so he and the director butted heads almost daily."

"It was on one of those occasions after the director

had threatened to send him back to prison that I became aware of just how dangerous Carl Stevens was. Maybe because he was angry or maybe because I was just an intern, he told me, the director was walking on thin ice and a guy who killed his own father, wouldn't hesitate to put a bullet in the head of a son of a bitch like the director."

"My curiosity compelled me to keep listening, and Carl didn't disappoint me. He told me that as a child, he had accompanied his mother to his father's mistress's apartment in Brooklyn. Carl was waiting in the lobby, heard his mother upstairs arguing with a woman, then, two gunshots rang out. Carl ran up the stairs and was the first one to see his mother's dead body. Somehow, the murder was labeled a "robbery gone wrong," and the killer and the weapon were never found."

"Now fast forward two years, and 12-year-old Carl was returning home from school; he stepped into his house and heard the same female voice that argued with his mother in that hallway two years ago. When he enters the living room, a very young woman was sitting on the couch with her hand on his father's crotch, which she quickly removes."

"She's introduced as Cheryl or some name like that, she was his father's new girlfriend, and Carl was told that she was moving into the house. Carl waited six months, and on New Year's Eve, when they were drunk and asleep, he slipped into his father's bedroom and bludgeoned both of their heads with a hammer. He said he ransacked their bedroom to make it look like a robbery. The police couldn't find anyone with a motive, least of all a 12- year-old boy. They labeled it a "robbery gone wrong. I remember everything about that dude."

After I told Phil and Marcos the story, I waited for their response. Phil blurted out, "Sounds like you knew him up close and personal."

"As close as I wanted to get. There's more, and this is the part that's interesting. I told the Program Director what Carl had said, but it was literally Carl's word against mine. A week after hearing Carl's confession, I arrived at "New Horizons" and saw several police vehicles and an ambulance crew outside the front door. I found out that the Program Director had been found beaten to death with a hammer and sodomized with a mop handle. Carl and his roommate were the only ones missing."

"Now, here's the payoff: Carl's roommate was an English guy named Donovan. Donovan was some superstar Ph.D. chemist from the University of Cambridge in merry old England, where he had the dubious reputation of inventing a designer drug called "flash flake," which, if I remember correctly, was a combination of LSD and cocaine. It became a sensation in London, and when Donovan tried to distribute "flash flake" in New York, he picked the wrong time. It was an election year, and just when "flash flake" was going epidemic, the FBI arrested him. His lawyer was able to plea down the charge and get him mandatory rehab."

Marcos joined in, "The police never caught them?"

"Not to my knowledge, but what you need to know is Donovan's other name, they called him" the doctor."

Suddenly, without warning, an ear-splitting set of alarms rang out through the confines of the Behemoth, sending a cold chill up and down my spine—

Phil turned quickly towards a row of flashing video screens that had suddenly emerged from a panel from the floor of the vehicle. He scanned them quickly and muttered half under his breath, "For the love of Mary, I don't fuckin believe it!" He slowly turned in my *direction.*

The look in his eyes was troubling; I spoke feebly, "What's going on?"

He glanced quickly at Marcos, then very bluntly, he said, "We're in the middle of Manhattan being tracked by two Apache Attack Helicopters."

Marcos turned away from the screen he had been eyeing and, with a nod, confirmed the awful reality. With a solemn air, he whispered," They're converging on our location."

I tried to mask the shock that had taken over me and asked, "So…we're being attacked?"

Marcos ignored me and yelled, "Ay, Dos Mios! Two missiles in flight locked on our location." Phil flipped several switches and then touched a button; outside the narrow windows, I saw two huge hydraulic drills engage on each side of the *Behemoth* accordion-like, each speared the ground. Within seconds, they had descended several feet into the cement. Simultaneously, a triple layer of 12-inch Nano- materials launched instantaneously, covering the entire *Behemoth,* not unlike the wings of a mother bird protecting its young from a predator. The next moment was filled with a deafening sound and the brightest light I had ever seen; then, everything went black and quiet.

Chapter V: Ball of Pain

The sun has made a veil of gold so lovely that my body aches.

Above, the heavens shriek with blue, convinced I've smiled by some mistake. The world's abloom and seems to smile. I want to fly but where, how high?

If in barbed wire, things can bloom why couldn't I? I will not die? 1944, Anonymous

"On a Sunny Evening"

When I woke, the room I lay in looked bright white and heavenly. I understood initially, that I had simply died and gone to meet my maker, but, as I became more conscious clearly I was in a medical recovery area. There was an array of medical instruments on tables and machines with flashing lights reflecting off of the bone-white walls. My eyes opened painstakingly slowly, they felt encumbered, heavily encrusted with sand and a sticky substance.

I tried to raise my arm with the intention of wiping my eyes and was met with a stabbing pain in my forearm. I looked for the cause and realized someone had implanted several large I.V. lines into the veins of my wrist. The lines branched off into several tubes that extended out of my sight range. I blinked hard several times, which helped to clear my sight, and eventually, through the haze, my arms and legs became visible.

Most of my body was covered with a thick yellow-colored salve, the kind given to burn victims. With some effort, I was able to make my fingers and toes move a little, much to my relief. The bitter taste of medicine floundered in my mouth. I turned my head toward my left and cringed when my eyes

settled upon the figure in the other bed. Marcos or what was left of him for all intent and purposes was a limp scarred body.

He looked dead. He was on his back, his face

bandaged from his feet to just past his chin. I shuddered from within momentarily visualizing the ill-fated Frankenstein monster chronicled in Mary Shelly's classic novel. The rest of his face was covered with fluid filled blisters of various sizes. What struck me the most was his scarred bald head, it had large peels of skin some burnt and all bloody. When I first met Marcos, he had thick black hair. Reflexively, I looked for Phil and found all of the other beds in the room empty. Suddenly unconsciousness took over.

When my eyes opened, Percy was sitting in a chair beside my bed. The rifle he held looked like nothing I had ever seen. It was a cross between an automatic machine gun and a multi-grenade launcher. I ventured to speak, but didn't recognize my own voice, "that thing looks like it could do some serious damage." He gave me a huge smile, something I had never seen him do, and then he barked out, "Welcome back to the living, Cuz!"

I tried to turn my head more in his direction, however, the pain in my neck was too severe. I winced and blew out several rushes of air.

"Take it easy Jay, you're lucky to be alive. You and that

guy Marcos survived two antitank missiles, them suckers hit point blank. Once our radar picked up those Apaches, we backed off and took cover. The blast radius was almost two city blocks. Even before the smoke cleared, we started digging you out, knowing ground troops would be coming to confirm the kills. Honestly, Cuz, we didn't expect to see any survivors. We dug into that mound of dirt, concrete, and metal, and we pulled out you and your new friend over there. Man, I got mad respect for that *Behemoth.* It got totaled, but it saved your asses."

I tried to speak, and the voice that came out of my throat could have been mistaken for the raspy words of a decrepit old man. Painfully, in a voice as thin as rice paper, I said, "What happened to Phil?"

"You shouldn't talk, bro. The doctor said you got burns in your mouth. They gotta heal." Words weren't necessary, Percy's deflection of my question and his eyes told me that Phil was dead. I was glad Phil was one of the "good guys," I wanted to remember him that way. I always liked him. Like Rick, he was only trying to help, but I was still here and I owed both of them. I didn't feel sad, I felt indebted.

I was impatient to get better and make those sons of bitches pay. The little bit of exertion I was experiencing urged me back to sleep. Hours later when I woke, I became aware of a voice that seemed to come from some faraway place. Percy had left the room and it took me a couple of minutes to realize the voice I was hearing belonged to Marcos. His thin weak voice beckoned me to come to his bedside.

Very slowly, tortuously, I turned on my side, managed to remove the oxygen cannula from my nose, and began the slow arduous process of pulling out the I.V. lines, then commanded my arms and legs to move. The pain was brutal, however after what seemed a lifetime, I stood wavering next to Marcos' bed holding onto his bedrail for dear life. I started to silently curse myself for leaving the sanctuary of my bed. I leaned my ear as close as I could to Marco's partly bandaged mouth. What I heard literally knocked me completely off of my feet. The last thing I remembered before I passed out was how high-tech the room looked from the floor.

It wasn't until after several days of moving in and out of consciousness that I fully understood the horrific consequences of the missile attack. The city was in complete lockdown, Martial law was in place and a state-wide door-to-door search was being conducted to find the two survivors of the blast. How they knew that Marcos and I were still alive was a mystery to me. Every hour on the hour news reports blurted out how dangerous the surviving terrorists were and constantly stressed that no man, woman, or child would be safe until they were captured or killed.

The fact that 143 innocent men, women, and children died in the missile attack was not a serious subject of commiseration. We were painted by the media as the reason for the collateral damage and that if we were not stopped, it was a certainty and a simple matter of time until we killed thousands of "good honest Americans." I felt sick to my stomach. I was nauseated by the depths of the *Clear Conspiracy.*

—The countless deaths flashed through my mind, rekindling the memory of an ancient song. It played in my mind.

—I was born by the river In a little tent

Oh, and just like the river I've been running ever since

It's been a long, a long time coming

But I know a change is gonna come, oh yes it will

It's been too hard living, but I'm afraid to die

Cause I don't know what's up there, beyond the sky

It's been a long, a long time coming

But I know a change is gonna come, oh yes, it will

There have been times that I thought I couldn't last for long

But now I think I'm able to carry on It's been a long, a long time coming.

But I know a change is gonna come, Oh yes it will

– adapted from - Change is Gonna Come by Sam Cooke

Those melancholy chords and words vibrated through my flesh, into my bones, and assailed my soul. Time stood still for this moment allowing me to cry and grieve. The need for revenge no longer existed in my heart. It was replaced at least for the moment with a lingering and enduring sense of sadness and desolation.

Several weeks passed and my mind began to clear. I underwent intense physical therapy. Marcos was no longer bedbound. Surgeons from *The Brotherhood* had performed several procedures on him, yet his face still wore lurid scars from that day. Marcos and I complied with whatever the doctors wanted us to do so that we could recover from our injuries. Marcos' face had literally been sliced apart. He had a particularly nasty 4-inch-long scar on his forehead which reminded me of the Frankenstein monster from the ancient classic Mary Shelley novel.

On occasion, we both chuckled about the resemblance. The fact that we could do that was reassuring and added to my hopes that one day this would all be over, even though I suspected the worst was yet to come. On the other hand, If Percy and the *Brotherhood* were worried that law enforcement would eventually come knocking on their door in their search for us, they never showed it. They gave us time to convalesce and as I became stronger, I worried about my future and Marcos. I asked to meet with Percy and his immediate superior.

The next day we all gathered in their huge conference room. Every *Brotherhood* member was in attendance. My words came out haltingly, "I don't know where to start, first of all, it's because of all of you that me and Marcos are alive. There's no way to show the amount of gratitude we feel. And, the level of medical care you've given us is unbelievable; your access to medical technology is phenomenal." Marcos nodded in agreement grimacing a bit as he ventured to smile. "But I'm starting to sound like a social work professor."

I wasn't sure how to say my next thought, so I just went for it. "We want to leave, we don't mean to sound ungrateful, but we don't want to put your organization in danger. There's a slew of law enforcement agencies looking for us and it's just a matter of time until we're found."

Until that moment, every one of the Brotherhood operatives had seemed to be hanging on my every word. Immediately, there was complete silence in the room, and then they began to look at each other. Percy was the first one to start laughing and slowly, steadily the room erupted into a chorus of laughing men and women. I looked into Marco's lone working eye and saw the same puzzlement I was experiencing.

I heard Percy's voice ring out, his apologetic tone was undeniable, "Sorry, bro, we owe you an explanation." A very serious-looking female nodded at Percy and with the slant of his head, he gave her the go-ahead. Her hair was jet black, cut short and she walked with an impressive air of confidence. Her catlike eyes drew in our attention and her voice was clear, reassuring and no-nonsense, "Hi Jay, I'm Mira, the leader of this faction of *The Brotherhood.* With all due respect allow me to explain, although I can't specifically divulge the source of our beginnings and resources.

Suffice it to say, that we are recruited, funded, and maintained by an organization of international power brokers who know the inherent harm of allowing a police state to grow and thrive in America. How do you think we managed to avoid detection for so many years? We are indebted to the two of you for bringing details of the "*Clear* Conspiracy" to our awareness. Your personal experience with the dying is the link we haven't been able to find. We're closer to finding answers, we need to continue to work together."

I felt frozen between reality and fantasy. I had always believed in the rhetoric surrounding the existence of mysterious groups of powerful people who orchestrated society in the way a ventriloquist manipulates a dummy. To actually hear it explained as a matter of fact, left me quite appropriately dumbfounded. I asked around and later discovered Mira was second in command of *The Brotherhood* organization. The involvement with *The Brotherhood* was both overwhelming and exhilarating. It multiplied my sense of purpose one hundred times. I shook my head while exchanging looks with Marcos. We sat down feeling the staggering weight of our new partnership with the *Brotherhood.*

We were two punch drunk fighters listening to Mira as she explained why our presence was sorely needed and how everyone in *The Brotherhood* felt the same way. I zoned in and out, and the last thing I remembered hearing was "Everyone would risk their lives without hesitation to help defeat the *Clear Conspiracy*."

The passionate comradery expressed by *The Brotherhood*, ignited my yearning for revenge. I was enraged wanting nothing more at the moment than to avenge Rick and Phil's death. I wanted to make them pay for what they did to Marcos. The possibility of those victories compelled me to soldier on. I made the decision to tell

Mira what Marcos had told me when we were in the recovery room. He knew the exact location of where the kidnapped people were.

For the next several days there was a heightened level of anxious exhilaration amongst the *Brotherhood*, it was born from their mission to torture racist cops, wage war, live alongside the *Methuselah* epidemic, accept the deadly reality of the recent missile attack, and the realization that there was a powerful enemy capable of annihilating them. The *Brotherhood* was electrified. There was a song being played over and over on the PA system. It became a chant, an addictive call to arms motivating and affecting everyone within earshot,

A large bell chimes slowly 4 times…

"I'm a rolling thunder, a pouring rain I'm comin on like a hurricane

My lightning's flashing across the sky You're only young but you're gonna die

I won't take no prisoners, won't spare no lives Nobody's putting up a fight

I got my bell, I'm gonna take you to hell I'm gonna get

you, Satan get you

Hell's bells Yeah, hell's bells

You got me ringing hell's bells

My temperature's high, hell's bells."

The song pierced the air, and passion pulsated in the music of the ancient AC/DC band. It splintered into my brain along with the rawness of the heavy metal guitars. Every fiber of my being felt invaded. The sacrilegious lyrics were a clarion to war, a beacon, taunting the dormant killer instinct in me. I made a silent vow to do whatever was necessary to get my pound of flesh. For one fleeting moment, I felt naked and ashamed of my feelings, but shook them off. Marcos entered the room and cocked his head to the side and slowly as if he was unsure moved in my direction. He stopped further away than usual and I forced a smile, his response was to step closer.

Before he could say a word, I asked him again if what he had told me weeks ago was true. He pursed his lips, looked down at the floor and when he raised his eyes to mine, his truth was confirmed. We walked (he limped) to the center of the facility where there was a small enclosed outside area. He stood there, a much smaller image of the man I had met several weeks ago. I asked him to repeat what he had shared at his bedside. This time my mind was clear and the pain in my body was controlled by the medication.

I stared into his working eye and listened, "El gente, el gente, the people, the people they kidnap off the street. First homeless, now everybody, women, children, no one is safe. They put the people in the factory for the *Clear*, Jay, I know!"

It was extremely disheartening listening to Marcos trying to communicate with me. He was doing the best he could. The traumatic brain injury he had sustained was horrific. I did my best to acknowledge him.

"Marcos, I know that part of it, that's why *The Brotherhood* is preparing itself. They've done their homework, they know what you said is true and they're going to save those people. What I'm talking about is the other thing you told me. You said you heard in cyberspace people wanted to kill me. You said they wanted to kill me because they think I am the gatekeeper to where "souls of the dead" live. That's what you said, do you remember?"

He looked at me searching for understanding, and

then sadly his whole face dropped and he fell into confusion.

Since the missile attack, Marcos' speech pattern had changed to broken English, he stuttered and strained to get his thoughts out, I never mentioned to him that part of his brain had been damaged and hopefully it was temporary. His lone working eye told me that he knew he had lost a part of who he was. I excused myself and headed to a back door that led to the street. I needed to decide what to do and who to tell.

I sat alone on a bench just outside the facility. It was my first time feeling the sun on my skin since the missile attack. I really missed the outdoors. The SCBA and hoodie I wore adequately concealed my face from the public. My body still ached, and sometimes the pain subsided, but it never went away. I watched people pass by and wondered how much doubt and ambivalence each of them carried in their minds.

I wasn't pondering the finite poetic aspects of being human. I was immersed in the reality that the majority of us live like sheep, pawns in a chess game fated never to be royalty. These were my thoughts as I watched Percy nonchalantly slip outside of the building. I was glad he kept his word and showed up alone. When he was an arm's length away from me, he stopped and said, "Whatever it is you got to say to me it's gonna have to wait. We got some old business to talk about."

I knew where this was going. "You forget the dirt we did?"

"No Percy, my conscience will never let that happen. I know what we did to Ronald. Sometimes, I wish I never called you that night, we found him and you almost beat him to death."

"Man, when he stepped out of that restaurant, I cold-cocked that son of a bitch, he fell hard. The way I remember it, bro, we left him all broken up and you had no victory smile. You pitied him. He hurt your mom bad and you couldn't take one swing at him. That ain't got no place here. If I put my ass on the line, I need to trust you gonna get me out before I end up toast, know what I mean?"

"Yeah, I do, Push comes to shove, I'll do what I got to do, when I need to."

Chapter VI: Promises, Promises

Mira, Percy, and Tony talked about every detail and nuance regarding the mission. Hours turned into days, and still, we talked about the mission, the plans, the contingencies, challenges, inherent dangers, and the reality of unforeseen occurrences. Now, the day had come. It was 3:00 am, and I was lying on the roof of a huge warehouse in the Williamsburg section of Brooklyn, NY, along with 8 others from The *Brotherhood.* The rain was coming down so hard that I could only see the muted shapes of the others.

The raindrops smacked down like hundreds of tiny hands playing timpani drums. My shoulders, legs, and arms still ached from the rope we used to scale the 70-foot rear wall of the building. I brought up the rear of the climb and, on the way up, whispered jokingly to Percy, "Why aren't we using motorized climbing gear?"

He shot back, "That's 80 pounds of equipment, bro. This is a reconnaissance mission; we gotta travel light and fast."

We had Marcos to thank for this mission. If parts of his memory hadn't cleared, this specific warehouse would not have been found. He began to remember details of months of research and surveillance he had conducted with Phil. Marcos and Phil put together some of the pieces connected to the people abducted off the streets. Marcos vividly recalled being on a lookout in Manhattan and seeing several men force a group of women into what appeared to be a taxicab van. He followed them to this very building, and before he could fully get his bearings, several shots rang out, breaking the rear window of his car, forcing him to speed off or risk being shot. That was only a few days before the missile attack.

I felt a tug on my arm, and when I squinted between the beads of water on my SCBA lens, I realized it was Mira. There was no mistaking her slight frame. I had grown to admire her. The *Brotherhood* held her in high esteem. It seems she was a retired army captain and sustained wounds so severe that most of her bone structure had been replaced with metal and fiberglass.

According to the story, she disobeyed orders and ended up saving the lives of 14 children kidnapped by a domestic terror group. They said she did it by creating a napalm bomb out of petroleum jelly and adding magnesium to the mix so that the burns became worse when water was added. She was captured, and most of her bones were broken beyond repair. I didn't get the whole story.

Right now, Mira was signaling me to follow. I crawled quickly behind her just in time to see Percy and the other 2 men enter snakelike into a hole they had cut into the skylight.

We scrambled over and peered into the dark abyss; I couldn't hold back a shudder. Mira caught my reaction and immediately said, "I'll go first, just do exactly what I do." For a brief moment, I felt at ease, but the moment was fleeting as Mira's SCBA and gloved hands disappeared down the rope. The descent was precarious, and my legs hugged the rope so tight numbness set in, so I loosened them a bit. I made it down, embarrassingly slow, but I made it down. When I touched down onto the concrete floor of the pitch-black room, I sensed anxiety among the others.

At first, I attributed it to their reaction to the slowness of my descent; however, I soon found out it had nothing to do with me. I turned up the sound on my ear radio and heard their chatter, "The specs on this building have changed, and blueprints are counterfactual. Is Jay down?"

"Yeah, he's unharnessed."

"Let's move out, Percy, take reconnaissance."

Percy spoke distinctly, "Roger that, I'll be two minutes out."

Two minutes later, in single file, we walked cautiously in Percy's direction. Mira took the rear.

As our eyes adjusted to the darkness, the room began to take form. It wasn't the huge empty storage space we had expected. It was the size of a football field, and it was far from empty. There were several massive metal vats lining the opposing walls. They were connected by soundless pumps moving liquid through hundreds of clear plastic tubes stretching the length of the room and continuing throughout the confines of the building.

My mind wandered until it was no longer focused on the factory. I blindly followed behind Mira, but my mind was years away fixated on the past, the day my mother was almost murdered. That frantic call from my sister Andrea all those years still haunted me. Her voice and words resounded in my head.

"Jay, Jay! He hurt her, her face is bleeding, and she's lying on the floor. I put a blanket under her. She won't let me call an ambulance. He trashed the apartment, everything is broken, and blood's everywhere!"

"Who are you talking about? Who's hurt!"

"It's Mom. Mom's hurt, Jay!"

"I'm on my way."

I was up running, grabbing my car keys, slamming the front door, and bolting down the stairs.

I startled the landlady, who was doing nothing but sweeping the stairs. "I'm sorry, excuse me."

Arriving at the apartment, I glanced at the carnage. I applied pressure and tourniquets, wrapped my mom in a blanket, and carried her to the car. With my sister holding her down, I drove 90 miles an hour with the hazard lights on to Methodist Hospital. After the hospital staff had done their best, I stood listless as I watched the surgeon walk away after giving us the "It's in God's hands now" line.

My attention was drawn to Andrea crying and moaning about how she had come home to visit and became suspicious when she found the apartment door unlocked. She had peeked inside and seen the mayhem then.

"I wanted to call 911, but she wouldn't let me. She pleaded with me, it's like she wanted to confess. You know how stubborn she can be sometimes. It was her boyfriend, Ronald. He did it, Jay. He hit her so hard, both of her eyes were fused shut, and there were teeth, actual teeth, her teeth, lying on the floor."

Andrea choked out the words, "Ronald beat her up because she found out that he had been stealing her money for months and using it to rent cars and date other women. He was having sex with them at mommy's expense." Andrea stammered on," She called the bank and found out Ronald had forged over $8000.00 in checks from her savings account. She confronted him earlier this evening, told him to move out, and he did this."

My sister sobbed, "He could've just left, Jay. He could've just left."

I hugged Andrea to help console her and also so that she could tell the rest of the story.

"Mommy said she never told us that Ronald did 12 years in prison for bank robbery. She didn't want to alarm us. She said that when he finished beating her, he bent down and held her and confessed that in prison, he had sex with other men. He said he wasn't proud, but that's how it was in there. He said he slept with other women to prove he wasn't 'gay.' Something about proving he was still a man."

"Stay with Mom, I'll be back later."

Andrea said, "Where are you going, Jay?"

I turned to leave.

She repeated, "I said, where are you going? Whatcha

goin to do? WHATCHA GOIN TO DO JAY?"

—*I turned my attention back to the warehouse,* silently cursing myself for allowing my thoughts to drift so far from the present crisis to a past one. I had to stay sharp and focused. Tony suddenly stopped and raised his hand. Like clockwork, Percy appeared and he didn't have his usual stony face. He wore an expression of uncertainty. I felt a chill run up and down my spine, as we waited for him to speak.

"I went about a thousand yards and came to a metal door. I checked for alarm sensors and found none. When I picked the lock and opened the door, I swear the room on the other side was alive. There were laser lights coming down from the ceiling!"

Mira chimed in, "Lasers?"

"Yeah, lasers."

I needed to know what else he saw. "Percy, were there people? What about the missing people?"

"I don't know, Cuz, that room's twice as big as this one. Even if I didn't have to head back for our rendezvous, the floor looked wired with pressure alarms."

There was a momentary low rumble of discontent coming from the others until Mira said: "I have an idea. Percy, lead us to that door."

Upon reaching the door, Mira took her time scoping the expanse of the other room. When done, she began to take off all of her clothes. It seemed I was the only one feeling astonished at her actions. Then, slowly, I started to get the picture. She was the smallest and the lightest. She was going to try and defeat the lasers and the floor alarms. We watched as she spread her arms and legs with her belly mere inches from the floor. Very carefully, slowly, she began to traverse the first few feet of the floor.

In the back of my mind, I expected alarms to go off, trapping us inside, but gratefully, I was disappointed. Like a human spider, she moved left and right, precisely placing each hand and foot carefully onto selected sections of the floor. At one point, her bare ass was centered inside two very visible lasers. Deftly, she moved with a purpose and artfulness that left me mesmerized.

The next moment caught all of us off guard. Mira's elbow gave in, and before she could recover, a laser glanced off her leg, and the smell of seared flesh filled the room. Everyone gasped as her elbow hit the floor, barely missing a pressure plate. She didn't make a sound, though it was obvious to us all that she was in intense pain. Her body trembled, but she held her position while her face grimaced in agony. For a full minute, Mira was virtually motionless.

She took several deep breaths, and with renewed vigor, she continued the solitary trek. Three minutes later, she collapsed on the floor after successfully negotiating the lasers and pressure plates. She lay there for a few minutes, and then her arm shot up with the thumbs-up sign.

She jumped to her feet and disappeared into the darkness. A full five minutes passed, and we were all getting nervous. The next moment, the lasers shut off, and the pressure plates lost their magnetism.

Mira appeared, walked over to us, and said, "Who's got my clothes?"

As she dressed, she explained how she had

difficulty finding the panel that supplied power to the defense grid.

I asked, "Did you see anything else on that side?"

"Yeah, Jay, I did see something, something I need you to help make sense of."

We began to walk and entered an alcove with various screens and monitoring equipment. The next few steps led us into a scene that could only be described as a nightmare gone crazy. There were rows and rows of cots with bodies in them. Closer scrutiny revealed men, women, girls, boys, and infants injected with IV drips.

As we neared the beds, it became apparent that the bodies were alive and had several tubes coming from them. One tube appeared to be for feeding, others were for excretion and urination. Mira knelt beside the body of an Asian woman in her twenties or thirties. She shook her and then shook her harder. The woman remained unconscious. I noticed 2 more thin tubes; one was inserting a fluid into her brain, an anesthetic to keep her unconscious. The other tube was placed in the center of her spine and was emptying what looked like spinal fluid into a plastic bag near the floor. The bag had another tube that led to a larger tube running the length of the room.

After checking each body, it was obvious that all were being kept asleep and fed, and spinal fluid was being carefully and methodically extracted from each of them. They were of every age, race, color, and nationality.

Mira inquired, "Jay, what's that tube for?"

I replied, "Someone's removing spinal fluid?"

Tony gasped, "What the hell for? That's some sick shit?"

Percy added, "Yeah, crazy sci-fi shit, that's real."

All I could manage to say was, "I don't know, I just don't know."

There was a junction box with at least a hundred cables and tubes leading into a small office at the end of the room. We decided to find out what was behind the door.

But, before we could take another step, we received a frantic message from the *Brotherhood* stationed outside of the warehouse. They talked fast.

"We have several heavily armed men pulling up to your

location. ABORT. REPEAT. ABORT the mission and proceed to t h e extraction point immediately. Repeat, abort, abort the mission."

Mira shot a look at Tony, who immediately typed into the small computer he wore as a watch. He looked up. Pointed to a staircase and mouthed the words, "RUN." We followed Tony and ran for all we were worth to the end of the room and down a flight of stairs. A lone emergency exit door stood between us and the street. Percy picked a huge lock while Tony poured an acid-like chemical on the thick metal chains. They melted like butter. Once on the street, we re-grouped at a rooftop a block away.

Through binoculars, we saw several men with night vision lenses and tech nines converge on the room filled with the kidnap victims. Two men with flamethrowers began incinerating everyone in the cots. We could see the flames through the windows. Three other men used huge hoses to vacuum the ashes into large metal containers.

We were sick to our stomachs. It was an abomination, the extermination of innocent people. The men had been sent to clean up the evidence. We had been detected, and the blood of all of the kidnapped victims in that room was on our hands. Our actions were responsible for their death. Mira ordered Percy and Tony to prepare to follow the trucks while the rest of the team returned to headquarters. Percy asked if I could come instead of Tony. Mira hesitated, then said, "Okay."

Being responsible for so many innocent deaths weighed heavy on my mind as Percy and I followed the trucks, being careful to give them a wide berth. We'd been following the slow-moving truck for about a mile when Percy realized we were being followed by what looked like an undercover police car. After a few minutes, the lone driver in the car turned on his lights and siren, pulled up close behind us, and angrily used his PA system to order us to pull over.

Percy said, "Put your signal on, start to move onto the shoulder. Listen carefully. You're going to stop the car and be ready to floor the gas pedal when I tell you!"

The police car was parked about 20 feet behind us. He pointed a spotlight directly at us which almost totally blinded us. He exited his car and approached us.

In a barely audible voice, Percy instructed, "Now!" We took off. The cop stopped, drew his gun, hesitated for a moment, then ran back to his car. Moments later we were being pursued by him. Adrenalin was pumping through my veins. It was dizzying. I glanced quickly at Percy as I raced around a turn, careful to maintain control of the speeding car.

"He's here to kill us; otherwise, he would have his lights and siren on, right?

"Yup."

We drove for five miles, reaching speeds of 120 mph, until Percy saw a sign for a lookout point and signaled to get off there. The left-side tires briefly lifted off the ground, and the right-side tires squealed, but I managed to exit and headed up to the dark, empty parking lot. The cop car skidded past the exit, backed up, and pulled up to the parking lot. He got out of his car and, with his gun drawn, approached our parked car and fired multiple rounds through the rear window and into the car. He changed clips and fired into the car until the clip was empty and then slipped in another one.

From our vantage point in the surrounding woods, I

felt safe and more in control, especially since we had guns in our hands. Our would-be assassin was a burly 6-foot-tall Black man, which surprised me for a moment. I remained silent as the cat-and-mouse game played out. Not finding us in the car frustrated the hell out of him, and he took a long look back at his car. He walked quickly to his trunk, opened it, and took out a black box with different size rings coming out of it. He turned a knob, and the box began to emit high-pitched sounds.

The guy entered the forest sixty yards to our right.

Percy whispered, "He's using a sonar box, like in a submarine. The sonar's probably picking up an animal, that's good for us and bad for him. Stay here, stay low, this is what I do, this is all me."

I did as I was told. Twenty minutes passed, and Percy returned with a slightly demented, victorious look. He asked me to follow him to a clearing roughly twenty yards away.

In the center of the clearing sat the bloodied shirtless man. Percy had laid into him good. His mouth was bleeding, and one of his eyes was purple, swollen, and shut. His hands and feet were tied with pieces of his shirt.

He was motionless and silent.

Percy said, "Let's search him!"

Moments later, I cried out, "Percy, he's a real cop! He's got a detective shield from the Jersey City Police Department."

Spinning around and looking down at him, I blurted out, "What do you want? Why are you following us?"

Before I could react, he looked up quickly and hawked a bloodied glob of spit into my face. I was still rubbing the knuckles of my right fist when he woke up 5 minutes later. I had hit him so hard it felt as though my hand was broken, but all my fingers were moving. He literally spit out 2 teeth and stated with certainty, "You two are dead and just don't know it."

Percy walked up to the would-be assassin, and just like in the movies, he broke the man's neck with 2 quick movements of his arms.

"Percy, we just killed a cop!"

Percy countered, "Naw, we killed instead of being killed. Best get with the program, Cuz, he wasn't gonna give up no intel. Come on, you can analyze this later. It's time to finish this!"

I joined him in the gruesome task of carrying the cop back to his car and placing him in the driver's seat. Percy found a huge stone and walked back to the cop's car.

"What are you going to—"

Before I could finish my sentence, he had hurled the rock at the cop's head, caving in the skull, causing the body to teeter, then slowly fall onto the passenger seat.

Percy said, "This sends a message to whoever sent him. It's our way of saying we're not lying down. Cuz, I don't know how all this is gonna end, but never forget, men don't fear men; they fear men who have nothing left to lose."

We made our way back to The *Brotherhood's* headquarters.

Chapter VII: To Know How to See

"Why you asking me? That's a dumb question. Who wouldn't want to live forever? Something like that gotta have a consequence, though."

Carl Stevens looked at his business partner and waited for his reply. He could tell he wasn't in a hurry to answer. Carl sucked his teeth and walked over the thick plush carpet to the window of the richly decorated penthouse apartment at the corner of 68th Street and Lexington Avenue. Carl Stevens was on a roll. He looked out and down at the hundreds of people walking on the sidewalk below. He felt like a king, sitting in his counting room surrounded by his massive fortune. The people down there might as well be peasants.

The drug *Clear, the cause of Methuselah,* had made him and doc millionaires a hundred times over. They had judges, lawyers, governors, mayors, and millionaires in their back pockets. The fact that a few thousand people were forced to give up spinal fluid was just part of the process. He had lost any iota of a social consciousness long ago. In fact, he didn't think he ever had one.

Ever since hooking up with doc at the New Horizons rehab, he had a new lease on life. No longer was he treated like some ignorant Black drug dealer. He dressed and drove an expensive car along with the best of them. He no longer worried or looked over his shoulder in fear of going to prison for the people he'd killed.

His father and that whore deserved it; they killed his mom and that asshole Director at New Hope. Shit, he had it coming to him for a long time. And that black coroner dude was getting too close for comfort. He could've fucked everything up. No way that was going to happen, Carl thought. Someone would have to kill him first.

By his lonesome, he'd been able to make a phone call

and order a missile strike in New York City in broad daylight; now that took some huge balls. The president of the United States couldn't do what he'd done. They would have made the President jump through hoops to do something like that. Yeah, life was good, and no one was going to get in the way.

He looked at doc and said, "So, what's this about living forever?"

Doc didn't bother to stand from his chair at his desk. He scratched his head and swiveled around.

"Before we go there, my able-bodied accomplice, allow me to pose a question."

Carl took a deep breath, then let it out slowly. He never liked Doc's British accent. It made him have to think too much. And when he started to talk as if he was in a Broadway play full of "highbrow people" like he was doing now, Carl could barely stand still and listen.

"What's on your mind, Doc?"

"All right impatient one, no use delaying the inevitable." Doc paused for a few seconds, "I never told you how I created *Clear*."

Carl's interest became stronger than his resentment, and he walked over to listen.

"What if I told you that I don't know how I did it?"

Carl replied, "I'd think you were joking or maybe using drugs yourself."

"Well, my esteemed partner, you hit the proverbial nail on the head."

Carl gave doc a quizzical look.

Doc continued, "When I nearly went to prison and gave all my money to the lawyer and the judge in order to make a plea to be sent to a drug rehab, I made a promise that no one would ever control my destiny besides myself. When we left that sad little rehab, I put my Ph.D. in chemistry in high gear. I spent days, weeks, and months in the lab working to invent the drug that would entice any man, woman, or child to the ultimate high.

"I did succeed; however, I overestimated what a single dose should be, and after administering it to myself, I literally dropped dead."

Carl let out a nervous laugh, "You died, whatcha mean?"

"Yes, I died. No, it was as if I transitioned, then re-transitioned into my body. I went somewhere, and something transfigured my thinking. I rose from the floor where I had fallen, took the van, and grabbed the first homeless person I could find. I anesthetized her and brought her straight to my lab, strapped her down, drained her spinal column, and added it to a special brew of drugs I'd been working on, and the rest, my dear man, is history."

Carl looked at doc with a quizzical stare. He knew doc to be a lot of things, but a liar was not one of them. He had way too much ego. Carl ran his open palm up and down his face, never taking his eyes off Doc.

"I needed a test case so I advertised on social media for people who wanted to become a millionaire. You should have seen how many blokes replied. I chose the two most desperate out of the bunch that responded. After I explained the procedure, they agreed quite promptly. I injected the drug into the cortex portion of their brain. Why the brain? I haven't a clue. It was as if my hands were being controlled by a force I could not see."

"Whoa, Doc, put the brakes on; you expect me to believe this? I mean, what are you saying?"

"Allow me to interject my own theory. Have a seat, won't you?"

Carl sat his six-foot muscular frame into a chair facing Doc.

"Where do I begin? Ah yes, thermodynamic theory, first. Let me simplify."

Carl took in a breath and let it out slowly. Doc noticed, chuckled, and then smiled.

"Contrary to popular belief, the first law of thermodynamics doesn't actually specify that matter can neither be created or destroyed, but instead that the total amount of energy in a closed system cannot be created or destroyed (though it can be changed from one form to another). For example, water can be turned into a solid or a gas.

"Christians believe God created the earth, and Big Bang theorists attribute the creation of the earth to the mother of all explosions. Whether you believe one or the other, both postulate that the total amount of energy in the universe existed from the beginning, be it spiritual or otherwise."

Carl complained in a bored, wounded voice, "Okay, can't believe I'm following you. So, what's all this got to do with how *Clear* works?

Doc responded, "Where does our body go when we die? It undeniably decomposes and becomes part of the original source of energy. Now, listen carefully. Where does the untransmutable life force in our bodies go?

"What the hell is that?"

"I'm referring to our soul, our mind energy, spirit, if you will."

Carl quipped, "Heaven or hell, right?

Doc quipped back, "Yes if you're a Christian, that's the deal you get. The overall indisputable belief is our soul or life force travels somewhere to be used again in some way, shape or form. Professor Jay Preston wrote a book about "Soul Repositories.". His theory postulates that when we die, our life force becomes part of a repository that stores countless essences of life or souls until they need to inhabit another living form or body. This repository is in itself a living intelligent energy force. Some call it God, Universal Intelligence, Mother Nature, or *shit happens*. Take your pick."

Carl's patience was running low, "What's this got to do with you dying, coming back, and creating *Clear?* That's what I wanna know."

Doc smiled and nodded his head slowly up and down, "My point is this: if Professor Preston's theory is correct, that same energy force storing billions upon billions of life particles is directly tied to this planet. As you well know, we have been slowly polluting and killing the earth. Our planet is so slowly dying. There are fewer life-bearing receptacles being born as well as others living drastically shorter lives. Can you picture, can you imagine the number of life forces being contained and desperately wanting to transmute into being, yet not having anywhere to transmute to? The natural order of things begins to break down."

Doc waited for Carl to reply.

"Look, Doc, we've got this far because I leave the brainiac stuff to you. I know my role, and I do what you tell me to do. Whatever reason you have for telling me this is cool. It's all mumbo jumbo soul talk to me."

Carl's phone rings. He recognizes the number, and a nasty frown forms on his face.

"It's the mayor of Jersey City."

Doc moved his morbidly obese body closer to listen in on the call.

Carl says angrily, "Why you calling me?"

The mayor answers respectfully, "I'm sorry, we've got a problem. Someone broke into the Brooklyn warehouse. We sent a squad in but whoever it was got away. We had to torch the evidence."

"Are you fucking kidding me? That's a hundred million dollars! I want names. I want them by this time tomorrow or sooner. Whoever it was, trust me, somebody's gonna die!"

Chapter VIII: 360 Degrees of Chaos

I feel free to be me. To cry of my own pain
to hide from feelings, to live without others in my life
at age 9 (going on 10), I found a place inside myself to hide
I remember scenes of rage resulting in,
that man forcing my mother's arm through a pane of glass
she attacked with knife in hand
blood splattered and scattered me into a ball of pain
you left me to feel free, to drown in my own pain,
to hide from feelings, to live without others in my life.
how can I unravel this ball?
Please, won't someone answer me?

J. Slater, 1984

"Hey, wake up, common, Cuz. Just because it's the 'ass crack of dawn' doesn't mean we gonna burn up daylight."

Percy's voice came from far away. At first, it sounded thin and whispery. As I moved closer to becoming awake, his words felt like an avalanche had fallen on my head. I sat up on the side of the bed. The clock on the wall showed 5:45 am, and I was still tired. When Percy and I returned from killing that cop, I couldn't sleep. Never thought I'd be a co-conspirator in a murder. I finally fell out at 2:00 am, and now Percy and Marcos were standing over me.

Marcos looked nervous when he said, "Mr. Jay, I have something I must do. I need your help and the help of your cousin."

I sat up, saying, "Hey Marcos, whatever it is, it's okay. Just tell me what needs to be done."

Percy added, "You better listen to him before you jump in."

"Go ahead, Marcos, tell me."

"Mr. Jay, this morning I find out on social media, terrible news." Marcos begins to cry out of his only eye.

"Take it easy, Marcos, take your time. Tell me what's wrong."

"I find out, I find out, mi madre, she died, died from cancer 3 days ago. I ask your cousin how I can talk with my sister and my family in a safe way. He good man, he uses special phone and I speak to my sister Emma."

The words stumbled from my mouth, "Emma, is your mother? Maria, Maria Garcia?"

Marcos dropped his jaw. He stared at me, speechless and clearly in shock. He shakes his head up and down and makes the sign of the cross.

I explained when and how I knew about his mother. He listened intently, not wanting to miss a single word of my hospice visit with his mother and family.

After I had finished, Marcos said, "Thank you Mr. Jay, thank you for taking care of my mother and my family. I was the one supposed to be there with them, but I was too busy looking for the missing people to be a good son."

"No, Marcos, that's not true. Your sister Emma said

you were the one they looked up to, the one who was responsible for everything. It's not your fault that you almost died in a missile attack. When's the funeral?"

Percy interjected, "That's the problem, Cuz, it's in 2 days, and he said he's going no matter what. I bought him in here so you could talk some sense into him. It is suicidal to think he'd get there, much less get back alive."

I looked at Percy and kept looking at him until he understood my thoughts.

"Cuz, you serious? Mira won't sanction this?"

Mira enters the room. "Oh yes, I will. You think Marcos came to you first? We're going to make this happen. We owe this to Marcos. I was listening to your conversation, and now that we know Jay has a stake in this too, its game on."

Marcos looked at Mira with admiration. The tears running from his eyes were hard to watch. Mira stepped to him, and they hugged as if they were never going to stop. Percy and I left the room.

The day of the funeral had come. Marcos and I

arrived at the Spanish Harlem funeral home in The *Brotherhood*'s van, accompanied by Percy, another male, and one female.

Percy entered first and canvased the area. He took a post and, through his radio, told us we could come in. Marcos walked in first, and a hush went through the crowd in the room. Everyone stopped what they were doing, everyone except Emma, who literally ran into Marcos' arms, nearly knocking him over.

This gesture allowed all of the family and friends to process what was going on, and they resumed what they were doing. Meanwhile, Percy and his team stationed themselves strategically around the room. When Emma finally looked up, her tear-soaked eyes focused on me, she did a double take and rushed into my arms. Percy and his team became anxious, and I nodded them off.

When Emma's embrace ended, I looked into her face and saw appreciation and telltale signs that she had found acceptance. After one more reassuring hug from Emma, I looked into the large crowd of mourners, part of me wondering if there was one among them sent to finish us off. Marcos was also looking and whispered in my ear that he knew everyone in the room and that I should feel safe. I immediately searched for Sara and found her near the restroom engaged in conversation with the chaplain.

She hadn't seen me and I spent that stolen moment lost in her beauty. I knew then that I was in love with her. I felt dismayed; then I felt a rush of panic, which quickly turned to shame. No matter how I tried to rationalize it, I had abandoned her. I created an inner monologue to justify my actions as I made my way to her side. Initially, we made small talk with the chaplain.

After the chaplain left and before I could utter a word, Sara lashed into me, "What the hell is going on with you? I haven't heard a word from you since that day with the Tomahawks! I've been losing my mind, can't sleep, I've lost weight. How could you do this to me?"

I wanted to tell her what was going on; instead, I played it off. "Sara, I've never intentionally lied to you—"

"What does that even mean?" she said with disappointment.

"It means, it means, I can't tell you the truth."

"What!"

"That's right, I'm asking you to—"

She quickly cut me off, "To act as if everything is okay when it's not? I don't do stupid very well anymore."

"What happens to you is important to me, Sara. Please understand that!"

"For now, I will; I think you're gonna need somebody who cares about you."

We held each other close, and the tension began to ebb.

We let go of our embrace after remembering where we were. "How's your daughter?"

"She's doing okay. I'm just worried sick about her when she's in school."

"You've got to keep her off the streets, it's not safe, not safe at all. She must remain inside always. You have to trust me on this."

Sara looked at me without expression. I felt as if she were studying every line, blemish, and nuance of my face. Without speaking a word, she nodded twice, kissed my lips, and walked away. I watched her head for the exit. Just before the door closed, she looked back. Her face was on the verge of tears, and she whispered. *I love you, Jay.*

Percy and his team were getting fidgety. Marcos had greeted almost everyone in the room. Marcos and I met briefly, and he repeated that he knew everyone in the room, so Percy didn't need to be so anxious. The funeral proceeded without incident and we had all agreed not to attend the burial. To do so could possibly put all in attendance in deadly peril. The risk was too great.

We agreed to meet at the van parked in the front. On the way out, I stopped in the men's room and after relieving myself, I stood for a moment looking in the mirror. I allowed the guilt and fear from the last few days to surface. It was shameful to treat Sara the way I did. Besides her deceased father, I was probably the only man she trusted unconditionally. The bathroom door made a squealing sound as it opened. It jogged me out of my thoughts, and I looked quickly to see who had entered.

I relaxed when I saw it was the pastor who had presided over the funeral service. He was a tall, Hispanic man in his forties with an athletic build and a winning smile. We made eye contact, and he said, "How are you, my son?"

"I'm fine, Father. Thank you for that beautiful sermon."

He replied, "Oh no, it wasn't me. It was our father from above who inspired me."

He smiled and walked over to the urinals behind me. Normally, a pastor makes you want to exude trust. That's the expected way to react. There was something not quite right about him. I watched from my peripheral vision as he unzipped his pants with only his left hand and fumbled to pull his penis out again with just his left hand. I would've ignored him except for the fact that most men unzipped their pants with two hands.

I stopped washing my hands and focused on him. There was a flitting glint of metal from something he was pulling from this right pocket, which caused me to lunge at him, catching him off guard. He sprayed urine everywhere as he raised a hunter's knife in an attempt to stab me. However, I was able to deflect his lunge and sustained a gash to my left lower torso. It hurt like hell, and blood flowed from the opening.

I was already on him and used my momentum and

my right hand to slam his head against the tiled wall. His head made a loud “crack” and then another one as it hit the floor. Blood poured down his face, reminding me to put pressure on my wound. I thought he would be out cold, but he staggered to his feet and reached for his inside pocket for what could only be a gun.

I didn’t hesitate. I took two quick steps and launched my body into the air for a flying kick. My right foot connected with his head, and I heard the sickening sound of his neck snapping as he toppled to the floor, and a small caliber 5 shot Berretta with a silencer slid across the floor at me. I stopped it with my foot. I had never killed anything in my life. Even though I was terrified and panic-stricken, I grabbed his legs and pulled him into one of the stalls, and closed it.

I immediately left the funeral home. It was a very sunny day, and when I stepped outside, I had to squint and cover my eyes. I started to bleed more heavily. The van was parked out front, and I slid into the back. Before I could say a word, the female *Brotherhood* members started giving me first aid. Everyone but Percy was there, asking me at the same time, “What happened?"

I explained, and before anyone could ask another question, Percy appeared.

"Hey, Cuz, I went to look for you after Marcos told me that wasn't the regular Priest. The story was that the regular guy wasn't feeling well, and the Bishop sent a replacement. I looked everywhere and saved the bathroom for last, and that's where I saw your work, Cuz! A little bit messy with all that blood and all, but nice work, and I got myself a shiny new Barretta. The guy you killed had letters to back up his appointment, so this *Clear* thing goes to the top of the church too."

The first aid I received also included a tranquilizer. When I woke up, I was back in the *Brotherhood*'s infirmary. The doctor approached me.

"May sound corny, but one inch closer and you would have bled out. You're going to survive, and you're going to be pretty stiff for a few weeks."

I sat up and winced, "Thanks again, doc."

Percy and Marcos came into the room.

Marcos said," Como esta, Senor Jay? How they know we at the funeral?"

Percy added, "Somebody's one step ahead, and that ain't good."

I was still too weak and sedated to get out of bed. I lapsed back to sleep and dreamt I was back at the university teaching a class. The topic was *man's inhumanity to man,* and unfortunately, I had plenty of examples to discuss. The class I was addressing was full of student psychologists.

"—In declared wars, casualties are expected and socially sanctioned. Law enforcement personnel also have this privilege. The number of incidents of a single person or group within a society that arbitrarily murders groups of unsuspecting people can be compared to an opportunistic disease process since the definition of a disease is: A condition or tendency, as of society, regarded as abnormal and harmful."

"Back in 1966, former U.S. Marine Charles Joseph Whitman killed his mother and wife. He then went to a tower on the campus of the University of Texas, killed 16, and wounded at least 30 other people. He was killed by police officers. In 1986, Patrick Henry Sherrill, armed with three handguns, killed 14 postal workers in 10 minutes, then killed himself with a bullet to his head."

One of the students asked, "Is that where the term "going postal" originated?

"The answer to your question is yes, that incident largely contributed to that catchphrase; so, what are your thoughts?"

"I think our ancestors were 'crazy.'"

"No one here will argue against that point. We have always been a violent species known to play out suicidal and homicidal behaviors. The Virginia Tech shooting spree involved the killing of 32 people by shooter Seung-Hoi Cho, a 23-year-old student who also committed suicide."

"Professor, I have a question. It's kind of personal, but I think it's relevant to what we're discussing today. Can you, as a social worker and especially being a hospice social worker, justify killing someone with your own hands?"

"Well, you're right. It is personal, as a matter of fact,

very personal. I think it's a valid point of inquiry, so I will answer it. Keep in mind that my answer is very personal and in no way constitutes teachings of any sort. If someone was trying to take my life, I would do whatever is possible to save myself. If that meant killing, then that would be my choice. Okay, it's almost time, class dismissed."

I woke up again, and the first thing I saw from the bed was Percy. He had headphones on and was obviously listening to something emotional. I had never witnessed him having a personal moment. Clinically, I knew everyone did to some degree. Percy was very good at keeping his "game face on."

He must've felt me staring at him as he whipped around and said, "Hey, Cuz, you gonna stick around this time? You've been in and outta sleep the whole day. I was thinkin about back in the day. Remember when you were around eighteen? You were pretty tight with that chick, your first love, if I remember right? Yeah, you were planning a marriage and having kids. Whatever happened to her?"

I looked right at him.

"You're talking about Janie."

"Yeah, I think that was her name."

"She died when she was twenty, I was twenty-one."

"Man, what happened?"

"Leukemia."

"Damn, that sucks!"

After Percy left, I used one of the "hackers and trace" safe computers to access my archives of Emails, pictures, and videos of Janie. I'd been saving them for more than 20 years. The moment I clicked on the last picture I had taken of her, the memories came flooding in.

—That day, I approached her room at the nursing home. The feelings of excitement and fear enveloped me, centered in my chest area, and became entangled there. As I turned into the room, she lay there quietly. Her eyes were wide open, almost motionless, until she sensed my presence. She quickly turned, smiled, and ushered me into a passionate embrace. Her hair gently touched my face, and I shooed away the fear I had brought with me.

Her name was Janie, and she resided at the Eastside Park Assisted Living Community. She was 20 years old, beautiful, sensitive, caring, and a brilliant painter. It was only 6 months ago that she was diagnosed with stage 4 Leukemia. My lover was dying, and there was nothing anyone could do to change that. God knows how much I loved her and would do and give up anything, everything, to gain more of the precious time she was being denied.

Last week, she wanted to talk to me about the blood transfusions she was receiving. In her opinion, they were a band- aid approach to avoid the inevitable. I sat at the edge of her bed and listened as she voiced her concerns about the psychological tug-of-war involved with the weekly transfusions she was receiving. We had come to the tough decision to discontinue them and allow the disease to run its course, not an easy decision for two barely adult people to make. The cancer had begun to spread to her brain, and bouts of dementia had become common. I didn't want the radioactive blood transfusions to erase any more of her. I visited every day for hours so that she would remember me.

"Jay, you know how bad my memory has been getting. I've forgotten how we met. Please tell me."

I almost burst into tears but held it together and hugged her, and for the third time in two weeks, I explained.

"We met online 4 years ago. You were sixteen, and I was seventeen. After a few online chats in the space of 2 days, we agreed to talk by phone, and after another 2 days and several conversations, we planned to meet. I arrived at your East Village apartment and, after being buzzed in, walked to your second-floor apartment and rang your bell.

"When you opened the door, I stood there spellbound, basking in your beauty, genuine smile, and natural grace.

"You said, "Hi, Jay, you want to come in?"

"We both laughed as I passed through the door and I glanced at you and said, "Hi, Janie."

"When you introduced me to your parents, we told them we had been friends from school for over a year.

"We left your apartment and walked to a pizza shop.

We talked for hours. I was amazed about your life history. You were born in Brooklyn from an interracial marriage. Your mother was from the island of Jamaica, and your father was from Iran. You have a sister and a brother and…"

(I stopped talking; Janie had fallen asleep).

I kissed her lips, saying, "Sleep well, my love."

That's when I took the last picture.

Janie died that night. When she was first diagnosed, she asked me to agree to be the executor of her estate and have Durable Power of Attorney. I knew her relationship with her parents was not as good as they all pretended it to be. I agreed to take on the role.

As per her wishes, there was no funeral, just a cremation, and her ashes were kept in an urn on my mantlepiece. Her beautiful art adorned various spots on the walls of my house. The rest had been donated to her favorite art museums. Janie's death took several years for me to fully come to acceptance. At age 20, I was ill-prepared to deal with the death of someone I loved so much.

So yeah, Janie's death was the main reason for my predilection with death and dying. That's the funny thing about hospice. You meet complete strangers at one of the most difficult points in their lives. The physical, psychological, and emotional impact is immeasurable. My place in the scheme of things is to help those who were ready for help and leave them with enough hope and strength to go on with the rest of their lives.

I continued to scroll down my emails and finally came to the one that meant the most to me. Three years after Janie died, I received a package in the mail. There was no return address. I tore it open and found a letter It was handwritten by Janie.

"My beloved,

It is me. I told you I wouldn't leave…my spirit is with you. My memories and my thoughts are embedded deep within your heart. I still love you. Do not for a moment think that you have been abandoned. I am the light. As you struggle to adjust without me, I watch silently. Sometimes, I summon up all the strength in my new world to help you notice me. I try to impress my love deeper into your consciousness. Please don't feel that you can't see me.

I am with you wherever you go. I protect you, Jay, just as you protected me so many times. Talk to me, and somehow, I will find a way to answer you. You are my lover, and I am learning to help you wherever you are, whenever I am needed. This can be done because I am the light. When you feel despair, reach out to me. I will come. My love for you truly does transcend from Heaven to Earth.

Finish your life with the enthusiasm and zest that you had when we were together on the physical plane. You owe this to me, but more importantly, you owe it to yourself. Life continues for both of us. I am with you because I love you, Jay, and I am the light.

With love everlasting. Janie"

Needless to say, I was in shock and couldn't rationalize how this could possibly happen. I had no real answers. Weird thoughts started to occupy my mind. I even looked in the other rooms in my apartment and, eventually, in every closet. I needed to get out of the house, so I decided to visit patients. I pulled into the parking lot of the Eastside Nursing Home; I realized that I had no recollection of the drive from my house to where I was now parking. I had been lost in my thoughts about Janie's letter. Once inside the facility, I walked down the hallway under the curious gaze of the nursing home with residents in various states of disorientation.

The average nursing home can be a moderately pleasant place to live or a rat hole for patients. It depends on resources and the attitude of the staff. This particular nursing home had limited resources; however, most of the staff had unlimited regard for the residents. I decided the first stop would be Veronica's room.

Veronica was 77 years old, born in Korea, and stricken with end- stage uterine cancer. She was a very energetic patient, and though small in stature, she had a tendency to climb over her bed rails and fall out of bed. She had face and head abrasions along with a spirit that remained undaunted and determined to avoid being bedridden.

After the first couple of falls, her bed was lowered to

within inches of the floor, and large, thick rubber mats were strategically placed on the surrounding floor. I decided to take her for a ride around the facility and began wheeling her around in her wheelchair, helping her to see the sights of the various floors of the nursing home.

We visited the 3rd floor, where we met a male and female Korean nurse who took time to speak to Veronica in their native tongue. It was a treat to see her having conversations even though dementia and pain challenged the simple act of speech. It made me feel good seeing her happy.

An hour later, I was approaching Camille's room. Camille had been a resident in the nursing home for almost 18 years, and visiting her room was always an enjoyable experience. We had bonded from day one despite the fact that the staff had warned me that Camille was a racist and hated black people.

Ever since I had introduced myself as her new social worker, the color of my skin had never been an issue. She never left her room as she was desperately afraid that a wayward patient would creep into her room and steal her precious possessions, which consisted of food items, pictures, knitted sweaters, and colorful quilts.

Once she saw me enter her room, Camille moved her head to the left and greeted my smile with her own.

She said, "Hi, sweetie, how are you doing?"

I approached her bed, where she lay watching a TV game show. I touched her shoulder and said, "I'm okay, I just came to check up on you, sweetie."

Most of our visit was simply watching television together sprinkled with conversations about her daily challenges and personal history.

The weekly visits with 85-year-old Camille started a year ago, and, in that time, she had confessed to me that she was illiterate and begged me not to ever tell anyone. I sat at her bedside, making small talk and watching whatever she wanted to watch. I still couldn't, nor did I want to shake off how Janie's letter had affected me. Her words wafted in and out of my consciousness. *You owe this to me, but more importantly, you owe it to yourself.*

When I finally left the nursing home, I walked back to the parking lot, opened the driver's door to the car, and slumped into the driver's seat. I sat there for several minutes, feeling the heat of the sun on my face, and eventually fell asleep.

I dreamed I was flying high up in the clouds; the people and landscape were tiny ants crawling about on the ground, unaware that they were being looked down upon. I flew for what seemed like hours in and out of the clouds, relishing in the feeling of being lifted by the warm wind and basking in the sensation of omnipotence.

Images of loved ones long deceased floated by phantom-like reflections brought home the reality of the losses I had suffered, bringing home past pain and feelings of loneliness. I withstood the emotional weight of this specter until a blur of multicolored lights resembling my beloved Janie took my hand and gently pulled me back to the ground.

My ears began to pop painfully, and slowly, I woke, opening my eyes to see the nursing home security guard tapping with increasing intensity upon the closed driver-side window of my car.

I waved my hand in a perfunctory manner and

mouthed the words, “Thanks, I’m all right. I was just leaving.”

Chapter IX: Resurrection

As a child, I was helpless.

Death ransacked my life,

taking my loved ones

and leaving me bare as boughs of winter trees.

No Spring would bring them back.

Plucked them away, without regard.

I was alone.

No telltale signs to follow.

Indeed, I tried.

Anger spurred me on to death's sanctuary.

I pounded at its door.

It peered out mockingly

and slammed shut my hopes.

J. Slater "February"

Two weeks had passed, and my knife wound was almost completely healed. Mira had asked for a meeting with me, and I sat in her office sipping on a bottle of water, wondering why she wanted to meet. It didn't take long for me to figure out her reasons. She reached into a drawer in her desk and pulled out a copy of my book, "Soul Repositories."

She spoke first, "Hi, Jay, how's your wound healing? That was a nasty cut."

"I'm almost 100%, still have stiffness and some pain. The doc said it's going to take about another month before I'm completely healed."

"I'm glad to hear that. You know, when I was in combat, we had to be prepared to have contact with the enemy at any time of the day. Sometimes, there were none for weeks. Then, quite the opposite, we'd have several in one day. You never knew when death would be knocking on the door. I lost a lot of men and women that way; some of them were my friends."

"Mira, I don't mean to be rude, and I appreciate your concern for my injuries, but I don't think you asked to meet so I could hear your 'war is hell' speech."

Mira laughed, "So you want to cut to the chase? All right then, I'm fascinated by this book you wrote 10 years ago, back in 2490. You wrote it as non-fiction and actually postulated a well-received and respected theory around it."

"You're referring to my *End of Life Theory*."

"I am, and more than that, I want to know how you came up with it and what bearing it has on what's happening to all our lives now at this moment in time. There are too many coincidences between your book and what's happened and has been happening in New York and cities around the world. Our intelligence is reporting that New York is not the only city facing this epidemic."

There was a loud knock at the door.

Mira said, "Come in. Oh, I've asked Percy and Tony to join us in this meeting. Is that all right?"

I responded with, "Hey, the more the merrier."

Mira motioned everyone to a group of chairs, and we end up sitting in a circular pattern.

Mira started, "Gentlemen, I asked all of you here today to milk your brains. Jay, for full disclosure, I ordered your cousin and Tony to read your book so that we're all on the same page, so to speak. They have assured me that no discussion about this book has occurred."

I laughed and said, "So, we've got our own little book club meeting?"

Tony responded, "You can look at it like that."

"All right, if you've all read the book then you understand the principles that are at work. If you've got questions, I'll answer them as best as I can."

Tony said, "It's not just the book; for me, it's more about what's going on with you. For example, how do you know there is an end- o f - life repository?"

"I don't, it's a theory."

Percy had been quiet up until now, and I could see he was getting anxious. "Cut the bull, Cuz, I know you. You've got some connection to death. Since you were a kid, something weird has always happened around you: sick people, people in trouble, or just dying in general."

Mira chimed in, "To add to Percy's points: we have police reports, medical notes, and some eyewitness interviews, but then again, nothing conclusive or definite."

Tony added, "One thing that's definite is your involvement in something supernatural."

"Look, the only thing I know is that…wait, let me qualify that, my research and experiences show that our life forces are immortal, humankind has been searching for the proverbial 'fountain of youth' for centuries, and it's always been in our possession. Essentially, technically and spiritually, we cannot die, not truly. In a sense, our life energy gets tucked away after our body deteriorates. It's stored and awaits our next organic form. We live forever, but we just don't know it. There's no recollection and why should there be?"

Tony gulped and said, "What, you serious?"

Mira asked, "Are you saying that women who are pregnant are incubators for bodies waiting to be assigned a soul or life force? If that's true, then who, I mean, how is it assigned?"

"That's one way to look at it, and as far as who is doing the assigning, that's elementary, it's 'Universal Intelligence,' God, Mohammad, Nature, Buddha, you name it."

Percy probed, "Is that what's been scarring up your body and then making it disappear as fast as it appeared?"

"Yeah, I think so, but honestly, I don't understand it."

"Jay, what I need to know is one thing, and it's not clear in your book?"

"And what's that, Mira?"

"Correct me if I'm wrong, but don't people who believe in reincarnation say that souls from a dead body instantly inhabit their new body?"

"Yes, they believe that. However, my theory is based on the principle of transmigration and the fact that there is a finite amount of bodies and life forces. Granted, in the past, transmigration may have occurred instantly. However, the significant reduction of newborns may have caused a shift in the equation. Also, don't forget

Methuselah and the resulting premature deaths. Not to mention the consistent patterns of war and the deaths from the inner-city Holy Wars. Something is causing deaths on this planet to escalate."

"Cuz, you saying something's trying to make things equal?"

"I'm stating that something has created a repository for souls or life forces that are virtually stranded."

"Not enough vessels to carry the souls, huh?" asked Tony.

"Yeah, Tony, and the larger question is what happens when this soul repository realizes that our planet won't ever produce enough physical states to keep the life forces in flow? There will be consequences."

"It's not unlike scientists that have been warning us about global warming since the late 1900s. We've been polluting the earth since the Industrial Revolution," replied Tony.

I said, "Yeah, it's exactly the same. Man thinks he's so damn omnipotent."

"Okay," Percy said, "what you mean by

consequences?"

I hesitated before I responded, "I think that 'something' is going to find a way to stabilize the process and get to equilibrium. What that is going to look like, nobody knows. I do think it's not going to bode well for the living."

"Hey, Cuz, I want to ask you a question, but I don't want to sound stupid."

"What's the question?"

"Okay, here it goes…do you know how to talk to dead people?"

Suddenly, a siren echoed throughout headquarters. Mira, Percy, and Tony instantly filed out of the room. I followed them and joined them, crowding around the desk of one of the *Brotherhood* members. An image of a very large building was being triangulated and displayed on a monitor. We studied the video feed, and undeniably, it showed hundreds of people being moved into a fortress-like building between the hours of 1:00 am and 5:00 am during a 3-week period of time.

Mira shouted, "Brooklyn again, it's twice as big as

the last warehouse. That's our next mission, but this time, we're bringing those people home!"

Chapter X: The Enigma

Sara was tired of being left in the dark. How dare Jay dismiss her concerns for him with such disregard for her feelings. One thing she had learned not to do was to stuff her true feelings. She was scared and angry almost every day now. Jay no longer called, texted, or responded to e-mail. He wasn't teaching anymore. She knew his sister and mother, but it made no sense to contact them. According to Jay, they hardly talked; they would be useless.

Sara was forced to act alone. She remembered Jay had told her, for the sake of her as well as her daughter's life, to act as if nothing had changed. She decided to heed his words. She cried again for several minutes, washed her face in the bathroom sink, and then made sure that Laura was still watching television. She thought about the handgun Jay had insisted she keep in a gun safe he had provided. She checked the safe and confirmed that the gun was loaded. It was getting late, so she started to prepare dinner. She still wondered where Jay was and what he was doing.

Suddenly, the doorbell rang.

"Mommy, someone's at the door!"

Sara went back to the safe, unlocked it, and placed the revolver in her hand.

"Baby, shut the television off and go inside your room. Close the door, Laura, do it now, go."

After she heard the bedroom door close, Sara walked toward the front door and then stopped, hoping that whoever had knocked decided to leave. She was startled by 4 rapid hard knocks at the front door. Moving in slow motion, she silently looked through the peephole. There was a tall black man dressed in a suit and a very large, casually dressed white man.

Sara said feebly, "Hello, can I help you?"

"Uh, yes, I'm Detective Stevens. This is my partner, Detective Donovan." Carl holds up a gold New York

City detective shield. "Sara, we were sent by Mr. Jay Preston to ensure that you and your daughter are safe. We just need a few minutes to ask some questions, and we'll be on our way."

"Oh, okay, just a minute, Detective."

Sara had never been as scared as she was at this moment. Her life and Laura's life depended on her next move. These men were here to hurt or kill. Jay was very clear about not trusting anyone. She felt panic overwhelming her and made a conscious decision to control it. She had the gun, but surely these men were armed too.

There was no way out of the apartment, and she had lost the key to open the gated window that led to the fire escape months ago and only made an unsuccessful cursory look to find it. She wanted to bang her head against the wall for being so lazy, so stupid. But there she was again, allowing fear and panic to take over.

"Hello, Sara, are you and Laura all right? It's Detective Stevens. We're a little worried. Answer us, please!"

She took three long, slow breaths, summoned up her

courage, walked to the door, and said, "I'm okay, Detective. You caught me in the shower. I need a few minutes to get decent."

"Oh, okay, please don't take too long. Jay is very concerned, and we'd like nothing more than to tell him all is well."

Sara put a large pot of water on the stove and turned the electric burner to as high as it would go. She pulled out 2 large serrated steak knives from her silverware drawer and placed one on each ankle under her pants, and used thick rubber bands and masking tape to keep them in place. Her plan was to catch them off guard. She didn't have a chance in an all-out gun fight. She walked quickly to Laura's room.

"Sweetheart, Mommy has to take care of something. I'm going to lock your door. I want you to play hide and seek. I need you to go into the closet, take your doll Annabelle with you, and don't come out until I come to find you. Okay? Do you understand, baby?"

"Yes, Momma, I do. Is everything okay? You look scared, is Daddy outside? I hope not, Mommy."

"No, baby, Daddy's not here. Mommy just has to take

care of something. It may take a while but do not leave that closet. Do you understand, Laura?"

"Yes, Mommy."

Sara took Laura and Annabelle to the closet, placed them inside, closed the closet door, and locked the bedroom door. She checked the pot on the stove and poured in a box of corn meal along with a bottle of cooking oil then stirred the bubbling concoction. She checked the chambers on the revolver again, remembering that Jay said the bullets were .357 magnums. Because of their large caliber, all she had to do was make sure she hit something, anything. He also said to go after the most dangerous person first.

Doc was getting nervous standing in the hallway, and Carl wasn't doing much better.

Doc asked, "Why don't you break down the door and choke the life out of her and the little brat? Wouldn't that be simpler?"

"Yeah, that would be simple and draw attention that we don't need. We don't have all the cops in our pockets. We have to be smart about this. Even if she thinks we're not who we say we are, I got this, trust me. This is what

I do."

Sara reached into her nursing bag and took out two hypodermic needles. She reached under the sink and found a bottle of industrial-strength bleach. She quickly poured some into a bowl and then filled both needles with the vile liquid. She removed one picture from opposite sides of the room and duck-taped a needle behind each picture.

She poured what was left in the bowl down the drain and put the bleach bottle back under the sink. Sara thought if she could get enough bleach into a vein or artery, a severe alkali burn or liquefaction necrosis would immediately cause nausea, numbness, tremors, a coma, and even death. She could not allow anything to happen to her; that would be a death sentence for Laura. She quickly filled up a teapot, placed it on the stove, and turned on the burner.

With the revolver in the pocket of her robe, she stopped to survey the apartment, satisfied, she said, "Coming," and walked to open the door.

Carl came in first, followed by doc. Carl re-introduced himself, and he and doc followed Sara into the dining room that led into the kitchen. They sat at the dining room table facing the kitchen while Sara sat at the other end with her back to the kitchen.

"Detective, you said Jay sent you?"

"Yes, he's involved with a time-consuming project and asked me to apologize for his inability to let you know we were coming."

"It's so nice of you to come over in person," said Sara.

Doc was bored and wanted a piece of the action, so he said, "Think nothing of it, my dear. all in a day's work."

Carl gave doc a quick glance, and doc non-verbally agreed to keep his mouth shut.

"Where did you and Jay meet," Sara inquired.

"It was at a…uh, drug rehab; I was doing security at the time. We stayed in touch through the years."

Sara was surprised at how calm she felt sitting at the dining room table, planning how she would keep these men from killing her and Laura.

Carl was thinking how easy it was going to be to snuff out this nurse and her daughter. Then he and doc would set up an ambush for her social worker friend, and game over. He wondered where her daughter was.

"Everything seems to be okay here. I was wondering where your daughter was. Is she all right?"

"Oh, she's fine. Right now, she's nearby at one of her friend's house."

Doc started to sweat and move around. Carl noticed and spoke up, "It must be difficult to be a mom during these times. With all the kidnappings, you can't be too safe."

"You're right, Detective. It's really tough. You can't trust anyone."

The teapot on the stove began to boil and let out a high-pitched whistle, causing doc to jump.

Sara said, " Oh, Gentlemen, where's my manners? I was in the middle of making tea. May I offer you some?"

"No, thank you," replied Carl.

"Don't mind if I do," said Doc.

"Would you prefer Earl Grey, Detective Donovan?"

"My favorite, much obliged."

This was Sara's cue to get up and head for the kitchen.

She didn't need to look at them to feel the scrutinizing eyes of the men on her as she jumped up and headed to the stove. Her plan was to stay just out of eyesight and draw one of them into the kitchen. After 3 minutes had passed, doc was getting impatient.

Carl turned to him and whispered, "Chill out; we gotta wait for her kid."

Doc took a deep breath and slowly exhaled.

Carl inquired, "Are you all right in there?"

"Kinda having a little trouble reaching the top shelf for the Earl Grey."

Carl rose and headed for the kitchen. "Here, let me help you."

He rounded the bend to turn into the kitchen, and immediately, his face was met with thick, boiling hot corn meal and oil. His screams were muffled, covered by the burning hot brew that was searing the skin off of his face. He reached for Sara and fumbled for his gun. Sara drew her revolver, pressed it hard against his chest, and fired 2 bullets that shattered his heart and lungs. She stared at the fist sized holes that were pouring blood onto the floor and jumped back as Carl fell forward. He was dead before he hit the floor.

It took Sara almost a full minute before she recovered from the shock and found the fortitude to step over Carl and head back into the dining room. By that time, the fat man was nowhere to be found. She held the revolver tightly in her shaking hands while moving around the apartment, wondering where he was hiding and waiting.

The lights in the apartment went dark. He had found her circuit breaker down the hallway. Fear overwhelmed her, and she froze. The apartment was eerily silent; before she knew what hit her, doc had slammed his massive frame upon her, pinning her to the ground. Her revolver flew across the room.

He grabbed her neck with one hand, and when he shifted his weight to get his other hand clear, she managed to squirm free enough to reach for one of the knives. She tried to puncture the subclavian artery in his armpit. But doc had too many layers of fat, and Sara couldn't angle the knife with enough force. She managed to stab him enough to cause him to roll off her and release his hold on her neck. She scrambled up, but before she could move away, he was on his two feet and had her cornered.

He punched her in the face, then held her dazed body tight against his huge frame and put his hands around her neck. The next moment, the apartment was filled with the sound of a child screeching at the top of her lungs. Doc whipped around to see Laura standing in the doorway, crying and screaming. That small moment in time was all Sara needed to lean forward, knock the picture off the wall, lunge for the hypodermic needle, and plunge it into doc's groin.

The alkali burn was instant. He shuddered with pain and fell to the floor, giving Sara the opportunity to reach to the other picture, retrieve the second needle, and plunge it directly into his jugular vein. He vomited for a while, and his extremities became stiff and numb. His body began to convulse, and his head shook with small tremors. He fell into a coma. Sara checked his pulse and respiration. He was dead.

She located her phone and pulled up an e-mail Jay had sent her weeks ago. Sara knew she had to put her emergency plan into effect now. She listened carefully to the audio e-mail and wrote down what was needed. She ran through the apartment, packing clothes, toiletries, pictures, personal documents, and every credit card she could find.

Eventually, Laura stopped crying and started to help. Sara was so proud of her daughter. Even with two dead bodies on the floor, she knew that working together was the only way they would survive. Sara could see the quiet desperation in her little girl's face. She felt proud to be her mother, but she also felt sad that what happened with her dad and what happened today would stay with her for the rest of her life.

In fifteen minutes, they were packed and hurrying down to the car. They pulled off just before two police cars arrived. They were driving to a location in Manhattan given to Sara by Jay in case of an emergency. They were on their way to the home of a stranger, a physically disabled former New York police detective named Dennis Gordon.

—*Back at the Brotherhood's headquarters,* I slept comfortably until someone shook me awake. When my eyes opened, Marcos' scarred face loomed in at me. It startled me for a moment, and I instinctively grabbed his withered hand.

He pulled back and simply said, "It's time."

I quickly remembered the *Brotherhood's* mission to investigate the armory in Bedford-Stuyvesant, Brooklyn. Marcos had helped me to prepare by cleaning my handgun, and securing supplies and equipment. He finished by checking the radio transmitter.

He desperately wanted to come with us, but sadly, he knew he would be a liability. Two hours later, Percy, Mira, Tony, myself, and twelve other *Brotherhood* men and women were scaling the walls of the armory. As a kid, I remembered riding bikes with Rick at the nearby boys and girls high school. The school had been a mainstay of the community for over 600 years.

We had often played guessing games, wondering what was being stored in this very same armory. Rick always said the armory was full of scary war machines, and I said the government was hiding evidence of alien life. The armory had been renovated many times over. Taking up about 10 city blocks, it was rumored to have sub-levels extending hundreds of feet down and had very few windows. The ones it did have resembled turrets usually seen on tanks from the 1900s. From the rooftop, I could see a full moon and the school field where Rick and I played as kids.

One by one, we quickly lowered ourselves through the skylight. When my turn came, I had no fear and quickly lowered myself faster than anyone. I said to myself, "This one's for you, Rick." When we shined our low-level blue light flashlights on the surrounding area, we saw that the setup was the same. There were huge metal vats processing fluids being pumped in from countless fluid filled clear plastic tubing.

We walked single file following the tubing as we did before. And just as before, we came upon a room loaded with lasers and pressure plates on the floor. This time, Tony came forward with a fist sized drone. He laid it on the ground, and it quickly expanded into a three-foot spider-like robot. Tony semi-controlled it with a hand remote. It began scanning the entire room and proceeded to walk calculatingly across the floor. It deactivated a 3-foot path, which Tony said would only last for 10 minutes. He reminded us several times that stepping outside the 3-foot path would mean instant death and potentially kill anyone in close proximity.

The robot took only 5 minutes to create the path. It wasn't easy moving our small arsenal through such a narrow path. Without warning, I felt 3 gashes open up on my back, and I winced in pain. At the same time, I had an enhanced awareness of my surroundings and knew to focus on one of the females carrying a large rocket grenade launcher. She began to lose her balance and would have fallen on the floor, essentially killing us all. However, I was able to brace myself and reach out, catching her full weight and helping her to regain her balance.

I didn't tell anyone how I sensed the fall before it happened. I had trouble believing it myself. I simply gave them a nod of my head when they said, "Way to go, Jay," and gave me a thumbs up. By the time everyone had gotten safely to the other side of the room, the gashes on my back had completely healed. The only signs were a few bloody smears on the inner part of my shirt. I was ill at ease knowing something had control over me.

We walked for another few minutes through the damp, cavernous space. There was a stark difference this time; a putrid stench clung to the air. I knew it to be decaying flesh, and I was sure everyone else knew, too. This realization changed how we breathed, thought, and moved. Every single step was being carefully measured.

It was dark, but we dared not shine a light; our movements had to be concealed. Percy was in the lead, and when he shot his hand up in the air, we froze. He gave the sign that something was ahead and then directed us to start walking slowly. Within moments, we entered an enormous space that seemed to have a life of its own. There were movements all around and the undeniable smell of death.

We turned our blue lights on, and almost everyone gasped. There were hundreds upon hundreds of bodies lying in the same state as the ones we found several weeks ago. Men, women, children, and babies were crammed together—wall to wall. Most of the bodies were dead and decomposing; the stench was nauseating. Bile in my stomach began churning, burning the soft tissue all the way up to my throat. It took some willpower to keep it from heaving out of my mouth.

Mira called out, "Hello, hello, can you hear me? Are you okay? Can you hear me?"

We turned and saw Mira gently shaking a young woman lying on one of the cots. The girl trembled, opened her eyes, and cried out, "Help, help me, please, please, please help me!"

Mira's jaw dropped and the next second, she waved me over. Simultaneously, we began to remove the tubes from the girl. I removed the siphoning tube from her spinal column while Mira tried dislodging the feeding and elimination tubes. The girl, seeing what we were doing, ripped the IV out of her arm, causing blood to spurt. I grabbed a large piece of gauze from my bag and applied pressure. The feeding tube was clamped inside her stomach; no amount of pulling would loosen it. We ended up cutting it and leaving a 6-inch piece hanging from her stomach.

She couldn't walk, so two of the *Brotherhood* men carried her small, thin body.

I took a long look at the entire scene. "Something's very wrong here," I exclaimed, " the holding area at the other warehouse was pristine, meticulously clean, and well-maintained. This place is filthy, contaminated, and highly neglected. It's almost as if creating the drug *Clear* is no longer important."

Mira stepped forward. "I didn't know if it was crucial, but we've been monitoring the street kidnappings for years now, and in the last few weeks, there haven't been any. That's never happened since we started tracking the data. I didn't realize how relevant that fact is until this moment."

That's when we all heard it, the unmistakable sound of ground troops moving fast and coming our way. Mira shot Tony a look. He typed a few keys on his hand-held computer and shouted, "This corridor, this way!"

Like a well-oiled machine, half of the *Brotherhood* followed behind Tony while two of the men carried the girl, and the rest of the squad armed themselves heavily and took up the rear. We moved fast, and the sound of the troops eventually disappeared. We had prepared several emergency extraction points. I became worried when Tony suddenly stopped running, and his face went blank.

"I've lost the GPS signal. We're going to the blueprints."

Tony, Mira, and another man looked at the blueprints that had been saved on a separate tablet. The sound of the approaching troops slowly echoed in our ears.

Mira shouted, "*Brotherhood*, set up a defense perimeter, ASAP!"

It took eight full minutes to get all the arsenal in place. Several large metal cans were strategically placed along the 30-yard defense perimeter. Everyone had automatic weapons, small grenade launchers, and molecular disintegrators, which, as the namesake suggests, make molecules unstable by breaking up covalent bonds, causing immediate death at the cellular level.

Mira was holding a weapon the size and shape of a football. It was vaguely familiar. I asked Percy what it was.

"Cuz, that's a *Brain Killer*."

"Come on, Percy, those things only exist in comic

books and movies."

"Is that so? What do you know about it?"

"I know it's deadly, thrown like a football, and when it lands, it sends hundreds of razor sharp shards of metal at the brains of people. The more brain activity you have, the more shards come your way. Technically, they sense brain impulses. According to the stories, the only way to survive a *Brain Killer* is to practically empty your thoughts and go Zen."

"You know your shit, Professor. We get intense special training so that we don't inflict damage to ourselves. *The Brain Killer* is a weapon of last resort."

Mira was barking orders; her tone was serious and confident.

"You! Get behind that column; make sure you have grenades. You four, fan out left and right. We don't want to get flanked!"

The unnerving sound of numerous footsteps surged closer. Everyone took their position. Their faces were not as grim as I'd expected, having the look of practical familiarity, which I could only assume comes from a life rife with military combat. I tried to emulate their preparedness; however, the closest I could get was a burning desire to exact revenge.

The sound of the approaching troops grew louder and louder until they were about 500 yards away behind a bend in the voluminous hallway. Suddenly, they just stopped and became soundless. That's when their faces became worried. That noiseless "you could hear a pin drop" moment invoked fear, something I had never seen from the *Brotherhood. The fear of the unknown was present.*

I could barely hear Tony whispering, "Why'd they stop? What's happening?"

As if to answer him, two huge paper- thin, partly camouflaged metallic disks careened around the corner, slicing through steel barrels like hot knives through butter, missing Tony by mere inches. One member of the *Brotherhood* was sliced in half just above his chest, and another lay mortally wounded by my feet. He was missing a third of his skull. I didn't know him personally. He started to seize, and I reached down to hold him to give comfort.

"It's okay, it's okay, I'm here with you."

He looked up at me to let me know that he heard me and that all too familiar "death rattle" ushered him into oblivion. I felt something dripping down my face. I wiped my face and found pieces of flesh and blood from the dead man plastered to my head. The spinning disks reappeared and took one more of the *Brotherhood* to a quick demise. It was surreal; everything seemed to move in slow motion.

Mira screamed, "Pack it in, head to ground zero!"

We took what gear we could carry and raced behind Tony who led us to a thick metal door leading to a metal staircase. He stood at the door while we helped the wounded and the young woman. Once everyone was through the door, he poured an acid-like fluid on all four sides of the door, fusing it shut.

We ran down several flights until we came to a stone wall. Tony joined us. "There should be a door here leading to an underground subway substation. It's been bricked over," Tony said.

Percy stepped forward with a wicked- looking grenade launcher. Tony pointed to where the door should be. Percy shouted, "Put your SCBA's on, step to the far wall, crouch and face it. Fire in the hole!"

Everyone did as they were told, but before Percy could launch the grenade, the wall exploded, sending stone debris in all directions, knocking Percy to the floor where he lay unconscious. Tony and Mira rushed to his side. As the smoke and dust settled, two figures entered through the opening in the wall. They wore *Brotherhood* uniforms, and when they removed their SCBA, I could see they were both women.

Mira shouted, " Zelda, Kim report!"

Zelda, the larger of the two, stepped into the staircase, wielding a lightweight weapon shaped like a cannon. Thick smoke poured from the barrel. The sound of the upstairs' door beginning to cave in caused everyone to look up the staircase.

Zelda replied to Mira, "We were stationed outside following the plan when four troop transports pulled up to the side of the armory. They came in fast."

Kim added, "And these things, these freaks piled out of the trucks and came inside. That's when we headed to the extraction point. Where are those freaks?"

I ventured to say, "What freaks, what did you see?"

Percy groaned. Tony and Mira checked him out and, finding no serious wounds, helped him to his feet. He was very groggy and would require help walking. The upstairs door was beginning to cave, and everyone looked up occasionally.

Zelda answered me, "I'm not sure what they were, we wanted to avoid detection and were pretty far away."

Kim said, "I know what I saw. Some of them were walking, and others were slithering. I'm not kidding, like they didn't have legs!"

Tony cried out, "We can do the family reunion thing some other time. We need to get out of here before whatever is coming down those stairs gets here."

I helped Mira support Percy; he was still quite groggy. Zelda and Kim led the way through the opening in the wall, to the train tracks, and through an abandoned subway tunnel.

Zelda said, "We've got about a half mile of track to go before we get to the main tunnel."

Mira and I were helping Percy when he suddenly

stopped walking, "I'm okay now; give me my gear, I'll take the rear." He broke out a formidable-looking rifle and took his position.

Zelda spoke apologetically, "Percy, I'm sorry You got caught up in that blast. Something was jamming our signal. We couldn't contact you. When we got to the extraction point and saw no door, we had to make an opening."

"No problem, Zelda. I'm just pissed we had to leave all those people behind again. We gotta figure out a way to get them out."

All at once, the metal rails shook from a heavy weight.

"Damn, they're right behind us," said Tony

Without warning, the woman we rescued started screaming.

"No, no, I can't go back! I won't go back. Kill me now, please. I've been begging to die for years. Don't let them get me, please…please."

Everyone looked at her. Her body was emaciated. It had no muscle mass. Her eyes were 2 large orbs stuck to a wizened face, and her hands had only a thin layer of skin. You could see most of the veins in her body.

"Place her on the ground, Jay. Do what you can as quickly as you can to get intel we can use," ordered Mira.

I walked over to the woman who was strapped to a stretcher. I approached slowly and smiled as I made eye contact with her. "Hi, my name is Jay, What's your name?"

She stopped her ranting and stared silently at me as if she hadn't ever seen another person before.

I pointed to myself, "Jay, I am Jay."

She put her hand over her mouth and pointed to her forehead. "Maggie, yes, Maggie, I am Maggie!" After she spoke those words, she seemed happy, jubilant as if she had a new lease on life.

I kneeled down and spent ten long minutes asking and repeating questions. It was as if she were 6 years old and had little concept of words and their uses. I noticed everyone kept looking back at the train tunnel as if at any second, we would be overrun by the troops.

Mira came over.

"What did you find out? We don't have much time. Fill me in while we get out of here. All right, *Brotherhood*, we're moving out now, right now!"

I took my time explaining my conversation with Maggie. "Well, it was like trying to guess a puzzle with a lot of missing pieces. I'm pretty sure Maggie was kidnapped 15-20 years ago. She knows it was a very long time ago but has no concept of the length of time. I tried to get some bearing on the duration of time and asked her if she could remember who the President of the United States was when they kidnapped her. It took some time, but eventually, she said, Elaine Jackson."

"Jay, that was 20 years ago. Could she survive that long in that state?"

"She said, at first, all she did was work and sleep. The work she described involved construction. I think she helped build that place. She was about 12 years old when she last saw her family. She's been in that building ever since the day she was kidnapped. She said she was never awake enough to speak, much less to get up and run away."

"So why was she able to finally speak?" asked Mira.

"You saw the condition of that facility. It's been neglected for some time. It looks as though whoever is behind this wanted all of those people to waste away and die. Something is not adding up; kidnappings have all but stopped, and *Clear* is worldwide. This isn't just about money, nor is it being orchestrated solely by Carl and doc. It never was. There's something larger, more insidious."

Kim yelled, "Look out for the third rail; it's like we're entering the active train tracks!"

The sound of the pursuers became louder; everyone responded by quickening the pace. That's when we heard it.

Mira spoke first, "Did you hear that?"

"A kind of rumbling, but from the other direction," said Kim.

In a hushed voice, Tony said, "Oh shit. It's a train!"

Kim exclaimed, "There's a train coming. We're boxed in!"

Some of us looked back and listened to the ever-increasing sound of whatever was hunting us. Mira was in deep thought. Holding her head in her left hand, she bit her lip and then shouted, "C'mon, run! Run toward the train as fast as you can and stay together!"

No one hesitated; we simply did as we were told. Four people were gently running, holding onto Maggie to avoid harming her. The rest of us helped the wounded. Upon seeing the lights of the approaching train in the distance, Mira yelled, "Run, run for your lives!"

We ran faster. The sounds of our lungs gasping for air echoed off the subway walls. Mira was constantly scanning the sides of the tunnel.

When the train was roughly a thousand yards away, Mira stopped and waved us into a narrow indentation in the wall she had seen.

She ordered, "Everyone put your back against the wall, take the wounded and Maggie. Put them between you. Hold them, and don't let them fall."

Mira checked to make sure everyone was as close to the wall as possible. When the train was 100 yards away, Percy and I grabbed her and pulled her to the wall. The faces of the train passengers were blurred as the train whizzed by at 90 miles an hour, mere inches from our faces. Time seemed to stand still, allowing a distant memory to take over my thoughts.

–The year was 2498, only 2 years ago and I stood at the

podium lecturing to my 6:00 pm class.

"One of the strangest burial practices known to man occurs in Mongolia. Lamas direct the entire ceremony. They decide the direction the entourage will travel with the body, to the specific day and time the ceremony can happen. Mongolians believe in the return of the soul. Therefore, the Lamas pray and offer food to keep evil spirits away and to protect the remaining family. No one but a Lama is allowed to touch the corpse, and a white silk veil is placed over the face. The naked body is flanked by men on the right side while women are placed on the left.

"The family burns incense and leaves food out to feed all visiting spirits. When the time comes to remove the body, it must be passed through a window or a hole cut in the wall to prevent evil from slipping in while the door is open. The body is taken away from the village and laid on the open ground."

A stone outline is placed around it, and then the village dogs that have been penned up and not fed for days are released to consume the remains. What is left goes to the local predators. The stone outline remains as a reminder of the person."

…I don't know why that specific memory formed and played out in my head. I guess I thought we might die. As the last car of the train passed, an eerie, uneasy silence took over. We stayed pressed against the wall, surprised that we were all alive.

The next moment, the sound of a loud crash, along with twisting metal and blood-curdling screams, filled the air.

We pulled ourselves out of the comfort of the indentation in the wall and jumped onto the tracks. No one said a word. They just reloaded their weapons, looked at Mira, formed a scattered formation, and walked slowly toward the still-screaming passengers. We switched our military SCBAs to gas mask mode to filter out the smoke billowing from the crash site.

Percy took the lead, "I can't see shit." He raised his hand over his head, then waved his hand three times slowly, up and down. We slowed to a crawl.

"No lights," Mira said, "we don't want them to know we're coming." Kim said, "How the hell did they stop a moving train? What are they?"

"Your worst nightmare," Zelda said, tauntingly.

"Cut the chatter! Percy, anything?" said Mira.

"Yeah, just making out the last car." He motioned for everyone to stop. "I'm gonna take Zelda and scout;

return ETA is ten minutes."

We remained vigilant and on high alert while we waited. One of the injured women succumbed to her wounds, and we were forced to body bag and leave her in a small area 10 feet from the tracks. Maggie's skin color was almost pale white, and her breathing was shallow. I took her pulse; it was hard to find, but eventually, I felt it.

Nine long minutes after they'd left, Zelda and Percy rejoined us. They were breathing hard, dripping with sweat, and uncomfortably silent.

Mira said, "Report."

Zelda reported, "It's a blood bath!"

Percy chimed in, "Never seen anything like that. Yeah, it's a bloodbath. Body parts are everywhere. We checked the last three cars for survivors. Something came through those cars. They or it ripped metal and people apart."

Mira asked, "Any sign of who or what was chasing us?"

"Don't know, nothing was moving," said Percy

"We need to finish," said Mira.

I said," Finish what? We've got wounded that need medical help, and Maggie's barely hanging on."

Zelda winked at Jay, "It's protocol, pretty boy. We gotta search and rescue."

"But there's nothing but body parts, you heard em…and if those things stopped a train…" Kim added.

Zelda teased, "You getting chicken shit on us?"

Mira said, "Cut it, we're all on edge. Let's move out."

Percy took the lead, and in two minutes, they had reached the smoking debris of the last car.

Percy informed us, "Ya gotta squeeze between the wall and the train. There's just enough room on the sides."

Kim said nervously, "You serious?"

Zelda responded, "You wanna wait here with the wounded?"

Mira took over, "We're not splitting up. Every man on deck, everybody goes. We stay together. Percy, you take half of the squad to the right side. Jay, the rest of you, and I get to the left side. You four, help the wounded and Maggie."

It was a tight fit, but single file, we were able to slowly squeeze along the length of the train. Inside, through the broken windows, crushed bones, appendages, and intact and torn organs covered the seats and floors. Suddenly, Kim vomited; her regurgitation spewed from the side of her SCBA, spilling down her neck and splattering against the broken glass window of the train, eventually trickling down onto the train tracks. She removed her SCBA, spat out the remaining puke, and then rinsed her SCBA with water from her canteen. No one said a word. Zelda grimaced and ended with a look of real concern.

Percy informed us, "I see the engineer's car; we're almost out. Feeling like a sitting duck."

Once we had all cleared the train and put the wounded on the ground, we gathered together.

Mira said, "There must be over two hundred people dead on that train."

I joined in, "Doesn't make sense. You can't hide something of this magnitude. The creators of *Clear* have been so careful all these years. Why risk discovery now?"

Without warning, my body shuddered, and huge bloody welts appeared on every inch of my skin. I could barely tolerate the pain. Everyone turned, stared, and was startled at what they were witnessing. The spectacle I was undergoing was short- lived. Suddenly, a loud, slithering sound came from the darkened tunnel before us.

They came out of nowhere, almost as if they were embedded in the wall. The tunnel before us was completely filled with the vilest of beings. They were huge with no familiar body parts and floated silently and effortlessly just above the ground. Moving swiftly, they were upon us before we could lift the wounded.

When the creature's bodies touched the wounded man and woman, we heard two loud pops. We looked down and stood horrified; our comrades had been instantly reduced to flesh, organs, and bones. Instinctively, I grabbed Maggie, slung her over my shoulder, and ran with the others back towards the train.

Percy and Tony got off a few shots, but the bullets seemed to be absorbed by the swarm of creatures. We moved swiftly with our backs to the wall, navigating through the twisted metal, revisiting the blood-soaked remains inside the train. It was a garish retreat, but it was necessary to avoid an instant death. We looked to see if the swarm was following and were relieved to see we were not being pursued. No one talked as we took turns carrying Maggie. We didn't rest until we had put a mile of track between us and whatever they were.

"I scanned those things back there; no vital signs, no respiration, no heat signature, just a slight ping on the radar. That means the only known way we can track them is by movement," said Tony.

I said, "I'm going to ask a question that may seem strange, but I've got my reasons, okay? I need each of you to tell me what you saw back there. What did they look like?"

Percy went first, "I saw lots of bones floating in a cloud of smoke."

Zelda went next, "I saw some bones, but mostly blood moving like a whirlpool floating in air."

Kim added, "There was nothing like that; it was different body parts, hearts, brains, livers, and what looked like veins and muscles. I didn't see none of that stuff you're talking about!"

"Mira, what did you see?"

"I saw what brain activity looks like on an EEG, suspended above the ground in a gelatinous body."

I summed it up, "So everyone saw something different floating in the air."

"What didja see, Cuz?

"Well, this is going to sound weird, but I saw the faces of people I knew who are now dead."

"That ain't weird, that's fucking creepy, just like those scars that came out of nowhere on your skin and then just vanished said," Kim.

"Jay, you owe us an explanation about those scars that appear on your skin," said Mira.

"I understand why they appear. Every time someone I am near dies, in my mind's eye, I see them transitioning, and I feel a force pulling at me as if it wants me to transition, too. When I'm very angry or stressed sometimes it happens. This one that just happened was the most forceful and painful one I've ever had. Something is warning me about death or end of life."

Mira's body became tense as she listened to a communication on her headset. "What's that HQ? I didn't get all of it…repeat, I said REPEAT! Listen up, everybody. Switch off stealth mode on your receivers. We all need to hear this."

Scratchy radio transmission was heard. It was barely audible, and everyone simultaneously turned up their volume.

Mira inquired, "What's that? Copy and repeat. HQ, I say repeat, repeat your last message. Headquarters were trying to tell me something, something about an attack. Then I lost them. Turn your receivers to commercial air. Turn them now, oh my God, this can't be real!"

Everyone had a quizzical face and complied. All of us stopped what we were doing and listened to the 1010 News announcer. He sounded hysterical.

"This is 1010 WINS, and I repeat, this is not a hoax or a test. This is a state of emergency! Eyewitness reports from both public and government entities have confirmed that the city of New York is under attack! I repeat, this is not a hoax or a test; anyone listening is being directed not to venture outside. Stay inside, I repeat, stay inside."

"The mayor and governor's offices have ordered every person in New York City and its outer boroughs to do what you can to protect and barricade yourself in your homes. Large groups of human-like beings are attacking the city. Thousands of citizens have been killed. If you are unable to get to shelter, use or construct weapons that can be used to injure or kill. The reports of these beings as well as eyewitnesses, have them numbering in the hundreds of thousands. Reports are sketchy; however, one thing is very clear: making any type of physical contact with them causes instant death. No one seems to know where they are from or how they got here."

"The island of Manhattan and its adjacent boroughs have been quarantined. Homeland Security, under the president's order, is activating all branches of the military, federal, state, and local law enforcement to enact Marshall Law to ensure that no one leaves or enters the quarantined areas… I repeat…"

We stared at each other, a lost, pitifully dejected motley crew searching for an answer.

Mira then said the unexpected, "Headquarters have confirmed the authenticity of the announcement as well as the existence of these beings."

To say we were stunned or in shock would have been

an understatement. We were feeling something very different. Our bodies were numb, horrified, speechless, and overwhelmed, oh so overwhelmed.

I turned to Mira, "So…what happens now?"

"The military can't use manpower to enforce the quarantine protocol, the affected area is way large. They're going to use cellular waves and fiber optic lines to completely cordon off the population. Anything or anyone trying to leave will show up as a blip and be tracked by one of the millions of war drones that go supersonic with a 100% kill rate. It's hush technology, and it's never been activated."

Tony agreed, "Yeah, that's the quarantine protocol, except they're not going to let the citizens know. Lots of people are going to try and get out, and they're going to be terminated."

Mira took a few steps to get close to me. "Jay, everyone in HQ except a skeleton crew is being ordered to the camp. Jay, you need to understand what's happening from a military perspective. There's an attack from thousands of unknown enemy forces we know nothing about. We need Intel before we rush in blindly.

We're heading to one of the camps in New Jersey to devise a strategy."

I shot back, "Camp, what camp?"

"Mira, let me explain. Cuz, the camp is in New Jersey. It's where we took the racist cops who murdered but never got indicted. We set them suckers free in the woods and hunted them like animals. Took some a few days, others a week, but they broke down and cried like babies. That's all it took; then we brought them back to sanity."

Zelda added, "That's a kickass form of behavior modification, huh, Professor?"

"Had a 100% success rate, Cuz."

"Let's keep it moving. The world's going to hell in a basket," said Mira.

We walked for hours. The GPS was not working so deep underground, so Tony and Zelda used maps saved on their personal digital devices. Tony kept the radar on his scanner on. He was looking for any movement, and at one point, he did detect a large movement. Mira ordered us into attack mode only to find a large pack of rats around the next turn.

Kim asked, "Where do you think those things came from? You think someone created them, or are they from another planet? Is this a small landing party? Cause if it is, and there's more of them, then goodbye, humans. Game over!"

"Really, are you ready to stop?" Zelda asked.

We finally reached the extraction point where a *Brotherhood* van had been left nearby just in case we ended up in this type of situation.

"This is where we exit. We're right outside the George Washington Bridge," said Tony.

Percy and Tony ascended 10 yards up a rusted metal ladder and together began to press on the manhole cover above them. The cover was rusted shut. Mira instructed them to go slowly and carefully. They were grunting, groaning, and straining. They had to rest several times. Finally, the manhole cover began to give. Everyone below started to look more hopeful as Percy and Tony dislodged the cover, and moonlight streamed down into the cold, dark, and foul-smelling train tracks.

Percy peeked out, “All clear, no bad guys…no people.”

Kim said, “They’re all hiding a n d scared to death, those that ain’t already dead.”

Zelda said nervously, “You’re working my last nerve with your gloom and doom talk.”

“All right, focus,” said Mira, “Tony, what’s the ETA on the transport?

“The satellite has our coordinates, and the automatic pilot in the van engaged twelve minutes ago. ETA is two minutes.”

Mira said, “Everyone, stay sharp!”

“I see it, the vans coming.” Percy said, “Still no bad guys.”

“Yeah, the van just pulled up,” reported Tony.

Mira ordered, “Percy and Tony, move out, search and destroy protocol. Avoid contact at all costs. Secure the transport vehicle, then give us an indication. Everybody else, stay focused. Zelda and Kim, get up there and get ready to lay down cover if necessary.”

Zelda and Kim spoke in unison, “Roger that!”

Percy and Tony bounded across the street, weapons ready. Zelda and Kim took positions at street level and canvassed the area.

Percy from inside the van, "We're in, didn't spot any bad guys."

Mira shouted, "Let's go, safe and fast, lock and load straight to the transport. Keep Maggie in the middle."

We crossed the street 2 at a time until we were all in the van. Zelda took the wheel, "Next stop, New Jersey!"

"I really freaked out," said Kim shamefully.

I said, "You just said what everybody was thinking. Personally, I needed to hear it because I was doing a little freaking out myself. I can't believe we're going to leave the people in the warehouse, not to mention everybody in the New York City area."

Tony asked, "Even if we could get them out, where would they go? At least they're being kept alive and…"

I interjected, "And at some point, they can be rescued. That's what you were going to say, right?"

"Hey, come on, Cuz, there's a lot goin on. We're all in survival mode."

Mira was on the radio, communicating with HQ, when she blurted out loudly, "GOOD WORK!"

Percy said, "Damn, Mira, what's got you so hyped?

She composed herself quickly and responded with authority, "We caught one of those things, one of the *Spawn*. They're bringing it to the camp. They constructed a radiation sarcophagus, dropped it on one of the *Spawn*, and it's holding it."

"Is Marcos coming to the camp," I asked.

She answered, "He's already there."

I added, "How are we getting through the quarantine zone?"

In a matter-of-fact tone, Mira said, "That's been arranged."

"Friends of the *Brotherhood*, Cuz, we got 'em in high places."

Zelda squealed, "Buckle up, boys and girls. We're almost at the quarantine point."

Mira stated, "We only have a pass to get through this one time. Once we get through, we're going to have to find a way back in."

Meanwhile, I was being as inconspicuous as possible as I moved toward the rear doors.

We had just crossed over the bridge into Ft. Lee, NJ. Tony was scanning ahead and said, "The quarantine zone is 300 yards ahead. It's roughly 200 yards wide, plenty of time for a drone to fire lasers up our asses."

Mira was listening intently to the radio in her ear. Suddenly, she said, "STOP!"

Zelda stopped the van, and all eyes were on her. Mira closed her eyes and focused on the tiny radio in her ear, fully knowing that all our lives were at stake. A full minute passed.

Mira shouted, "Zelda, go! We've got 30 seconds to get to the other side of the quarantined area."

Zelda punched the accelerator, and at the same time, I grabbed a duffle bag of weapons and supplies, pushed open the rear door, and fell to the ground, rolling several times until I came to a stop. Everyone was in disbelief, totally taken by surprise. I could hear Percy yelling, "NO!" He yelled it several times.

He sprinted toward the back of the van, but

before he could launch himself, he was restrained by 3 members of the *Brotherhood.* He struggled, but to no avail. They held him down.

Mira yelled, "Keep going, don't stop, keep going, or we're all dead meat!"

I stood up and saw the van drive safely through the quarantine zone. They all looked back, and I gave them a military salute. I picked up the guns and supplies. Quickly, I headed in the direction of Manhattan.

—A single killer drone shot over the sky, hovered for a few seconds, then quickly disappeared.

END OF PART ONE

About the Author

Art Jetthree is a laid-back guy. He has worked with vulnerable populations throughout his career as a clinical social worker and university Professor. He has a strong proclivity toward the unknown elements of life on earth and in this universe. He is a Thai Chi instructor and a lifelong martial artist. He is grateful to have an empathetic and understanding nature towards our planet, individuals and families struggling to survive. His lifelong perspectives are founded on the principle and value of "knowing how to see." The Clear Conspiracy" is his first set of fiction books.

www.ingramcontent.com/pod-product-compliance
Ingram Content Group UK Ltd.
Pitfield, Milton Keynes, MK11 3LW, UK
UKHW062254290726
14090UKWH00017B/672